Carolyn Denn

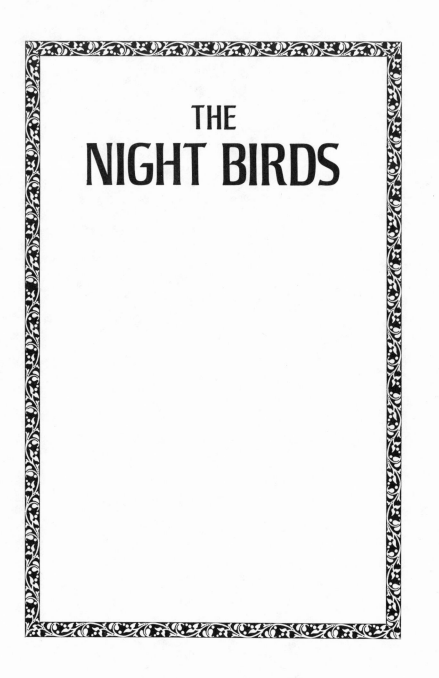

# THE
# NIGHT BIRDS

# THE
# NIGHT BIRDS

## TORMOD HAUGEN
### Translated from the Norwegian
### by Sheila La Farge

*A Merloyd Lawrence Book*
DELACORTE PRESS/SEYMOUR LAWRENCE

*A MERLOYD LAWRENCE BOOK*
Published by
Delacorte Press / Seymour Lawrence
1 Dag Hammarskjold Plaza
New York, N.Y. 10017


This work was first published in Norway
by Gyldendal Norsk Forlag as NATTFUGLENE.
⁎ © Gyldendal Norsk Forlag A/S 1975.

Translation copyright © 1982 by Dell Publishing Co., Inc.

Manufactured in the United States of America
First printing

Design by Jordan Brener

LIBRARY OF CONGRESS CATALOGING IN PUBLICATION DATA

Haugen, Tormod.
The night birds.
Translation of: Nattfuglene.
"A Merloyd Lawrence Book."
Summary: Jake struggles to come to grip with terrors
real and imagined, including his father's bouts of
depression and his own nightmares.
[1. Emotional problems—Fiction] I. Title.
PZ7.H2866Ni        [Fic]        82–70311
ISBN 0–440–06451–1              AACR2
ISBN 0–440–06452–X (lib. bdg.)

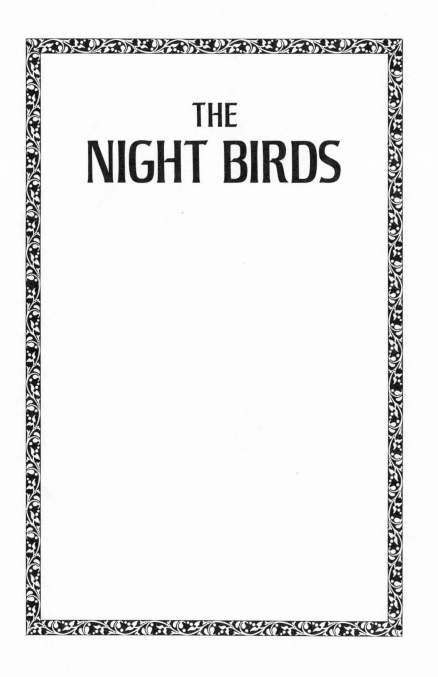

# THE
# NIGHT BIRDS

# One

Don't make a sound on the stairs.

Sneak past the big, worn brown spot on the fourth step. Whisper softly to yourself, "Abracadabra, I'm free." Hold your breath till you get to the first landing where the stairs turn. Then the spot has no more power over you.

Duck down past the dangerous door with the dangerous peephole.

An eye.

A big, bright, staring eye that never blinks. It looks and looks and looks. Night and day. It looks at everyone who goes by.

A witch's eye.

One day that door might suddenly burst open and he might not make it past. A voice would shout, "Abracadabra, now I've got you!"

The witch, Mrs. Andersen, was waiting to grab him, pull him into her front hall and shut him up in a cage. A narrow little cage where he'd have to stay until he got to be an old man with white hair and a beard and a cane and sciatica like Grandad.

That's what Sara said.

Hurry upstairs, round the turn. Don't make a sound. Let your breath out gently at the second floor, lean over the banister, and look down at the witch's door.

He had to look down every time he went upstairs, he couldn't help it. Every once in a while he had to say something, even shout. Once he shouted some rubbish so loud that Karlsen on the second floor came rushing out to see what was up.

He forgot that other people could hear him.

He was afraid of Karlsen, who had such fierce eyebrows. They were messy, like a worn-out brush, and he also had a dangerous, booming voice.

At one time he believed Karlsen was God.

Sara was the one who told him that, but Mom said it wasn't really true.

Next door to Karlsen lived the mysterious people, and he was scared of them too.

A nameplate on the door. It said Skogli, but no one lived there, or at least he'd never seen anyone come out of there.

He was sure that something stood right inside, with gigantically large ears pressed to the door: something was there; he didn't know what, only that it was big and black and dangerous with enormous, flapping ears.

It was so silent behind the door that he could tell something was there.

Once Mom went down to visit the Skoglis. This made him so worried that he had to go pee. He wanted to tell her it was dangerous to visit the spooks even if they did call themselves Skogli, but he couldn't get a word out. His whole throat was dry.

Anyway, Mom came back up after a while, and she wasn't at all different. She brought a book with her that she'd borrowed from the spooks. It was an absolutely ordinary book, nothing suspicious about it in any way.

If he got safely past that brown spot (and he always had so far) and passed witch Andersen's door (he'd always done that too) and wasn't stopped by Karlsen, he had to walk right over to the spooks' door.

He really wanted to run right past, but every time he slowed down instead. Even though he was so scared that he heard his heartbeat echoing in the stairwell, he had to walk over to the door and put his ear up against it.

And then—just before the door would open and the ears come flapping out—he'd run just as fast as he could up to the next floor. Then he was safe, because his own door was there.

Hansen was written on the nameplate. Erik, Linda, and Jake Hansen.

Erik was his dad. Linda was Mom, and Jake was himself.

Once he saw the nameplate, he felt safe. Then he was out of danger, though Sara said dangers were lurking everywhere, so he shouldn't be too sure.

The Rudds lived next door, and they were nice. He

often went there and got good things to eat. They had a little baby who was just a few months old, and it was neat to see him yell. His face turned all red and wrinkly.

Sara was sure there was something suspicious about them at night. They'd probably made a secret door to get into Jake and his parents' place and were waiting to steal everything.

Jake had looked for it, but there was no secret door.

"Then they're probably making one," said Sara.

As for the fourth floor, he didn't know who lived there. It didn't matter, because he'd never been there, and he wasn't going either. Because you never know, which was what both Sara and Dad said.

Safely back at his door.

Shouting on the stairs was not allowed.

But he was getting strong from passing all the dangers safely. He was getting brave.

He unlocked the door, shouted "FATHER" so loud that it echoed down the stairs. Then he dashed in and closed the door before anyone could poke a head out and glare at him furiously.

# TWO

The door closed behind him with a sigh.

"Daddy!"

He didn't have to say FATHER when he was home, because no one dangerous could hear him.

No one answered.

That wasn't strange. Dad was often so busy with his own thoughts that he didn't hear.

He dropped his schoolbag on the floor although he really should have taken it straight to his own room.

He kicked off his boots and left them lying in a heap although he really should have put them neatly side by side on the metal stand under the hat rack.

He ran into the living room, dragging the front hall rug with him to the threshold, but he didn't bother about that either.

No one in the living room.

"Dad!"

His voice shrank to nothing in the empty room and he hurried back out into the front hall.

"Erik!"

No one answered.

He looked around, and then he realized no one was home.

The vacuum cleaner sat in the middle of the living room floor. Dad had promised to really clean the place up today because Jan and Willy were to come over in the evening.

On the kitchen counter were all the dirty dishes in a pile that was growing and growing every day; the lowest plates in the pile were four days old.

"Now we don't have anything left to eat off," Mom had said this morning.

"Okay," said Dad, "I *will* do the dishes today."

"You said that yesterday too," Mom replied.

"But today I'll do it," said Dad.

In the bedroom the curtains hadn't been pulled. It smelled sour and stuffy, of nighttime, and the beds were a mess of untidy quilts.

It was dark in Jake's room too.

No Dad. He hadn't done anything all day.

Jake started to worry. He'd expected Dad to be home because he'd promised to be there.

Dad had laughed and joked at breakfast, so something bad must have happened during the day since he hadn't got anything done at all.

Jake stood in the front hall again.

Dad's boots were there. His good shoes too. His wooden clogs were gone. That meant he wasn't going very far.

His coat was hanging there. His leather jacket too. It was his Windbreaker that was missing. He used that when he was going to walk a very long way.

Wooden clogs and a Windbreaker.

Nearby and far.

It didn't make sense.

Jake frowned. Dad must be having a terrible time today.

He sighed. It was difficult having a dad who was difficult.

His good mood completely disappeared. He'd been so sure Dad would be there.

Now there seemed no point in being in the house alone.

He wanted to go out and look for Dad. But where in the world should he look?

Clogs and a Windbreaker.

Really wacky.

Jake pulled on his boots again and slammed the door behind him.

# Three

He stopped on the sidewalk in front of the house. The street was black with rain from earlier in the day. The sun had come out and glittered a little in the gutters. A faint slushing sound came from wheels as cars drove past. Like whispering. He was glad there wasn't much water in the gutters because then it was so easy to get splashed.

He was lucky to live on this street. It didn't have much traffic. Of course you could see cars almost all the time, but they didn't come so close together and there weren't as many as in streets with real traffic.

On one side of the street stood the old houses that had apartments with high ceilings. All the buildings had four floors and were the same height. Luckily the colors of the houses were different.

Jake lived in Number Thirty-five, which was a neat number.

A bakery, a tobacco shop, and a little corner store were the only shops on this block. The corner store would be closing down soon. Just a couple of blocks away there was a supermarket and a new, modern department store.

Across the street was the park.

Not every street had a park, so that was another reason he was lucky to live on that street. They were allowed to play anywhere in the park even though it had a playground.

Where should he go?

Jake looked up and down the street. There weren't many people in sight and no one who looked like Dad.

Tommy came out from next door. Sometimes he would act as if he knew Jake. Tommy was in third grade; he was a year older than Jake.

Tommy looked at him, which meant that he knew him right at this moment, at least until any bigger kids came along.

"Have you seen my daddy?" asked Jake.

"Your daddy?" Tommy gaped at him. "God, I didn't know people had daddies."

Jake winced. He'd forgotten. You can't say Mommy and Daddy away from home.

"I mean, have you seen my father?" said Jake, starting again, trying to sound as if he hadn't heard what Tommy had just said.

"Your old man? Why didn't you say that right away? I didn't know you were a baby."

"I'm not," said Jake.

"Then why did you ask if I'd seen your daddy?"

"I asked if you'd seen my father."

Tommy came right up to him and spat just in front of his feet.

"Watch out or I'll spit between your freckles. I know exactly what you said, don't I?"

Jake looked down. "Yes," he whispered.

"Right," said Tommy. "I haven't seen your father."

Then he turned and walked away. Jake watched him go. Tommy shouted over his shoulder, "You ought to get a better name for your daddy if you ever find him."

Then he ran off.

Watching him go, Jake crossed his fingers and said to himself, "Hocus-pocus, words and nerds, you'll turn into little turds."

You had to cross your fingers, Sara said, or else it wouldn't work.

Dumb Tommy.

Jake took a good look around, then he ran across the street and into the park.

# Four

The park was square and green.

Some black asphalt paths crossing the grass were ugly to look at.

There were trees and bushes in the park, green and

dense in summer; in winter they were stiff and black.

When Jake stood under the leafy maples in summer and looked up, the sky was green and the birds were heavenly birds singing heavenly songs.

In winter the sky was gray or blue above the same maple trees.

On dark evenings before all the leaves fell off, the bushes were full of hiding places. It was creepy walking near the bushes after dark, because they were full of odd noises.

In summer the park was crowded with baby carriages and people sunning themselves on the grass and red benches were put out all around.

The park was full of noises. Mostly kids' noise from the playground. And the wind lived in the big treetops. He could both see and hear it.

The treetops were still thick with leaves, but they had begun to fall and change color.

It was September in the park.

Late September.

# Five

Maybe Dad was in the park.

Maybe he wasn't.

There was absolutely no way of knowing when he was wearing both clogs and a Windbreaker.

Why a Windbreaker, when fall hadn't even really started yet?

There was a slight breeze. Sometimes he felt raindrops on his face. The trees teased him.

The paths went in all directions. He didn't know how many there were. Many too many when he didn't know which way to go.

Dad could have gone anywhere.

Dumb Dad.

Why couldn't he write a note saying where he was!

"Remember to write a note to say where you are, if you won't be home when I get back from work," Mom would say to Jake.

He had to do that or they'd worry about him.

But Dad didn't have to. He was grown up, after all. Didn't Dad ever think that Jake might worry about his dad?

It was dumb that Dad had to be like that.

He hadn't been like that while he was studying to be a teacher, but then the third day after Dad started teaching in the junior high that fall, he came home and said he couldn't handle it.

Dad sat at the kitchen table almost crying when he told about how awful it had been. "There was a glass wall between me and the kids," he said. "And I got scared. The kids knew it, and then I got even more scared. It won't work," he said.

So Dad was given sick leave. His nerves failed.

Fritz, the doctor Mom and Dad knew, said he should stay home awhile and take it easy. Then perhaps in the middle of October . . . "Yes," said Dad, "then I can start again."

But Dad's nerves hadn't gotten better.

When he felt too miserable, he would clear out and might be gone until late at night.

Jake clenched his fists and his teeth. He almost felt he had to cry when he thought about Dad's nerves. They made Dad so different from the way he used to be.

But then he caught sight of Julie and Tora walking toward him. Jake stuck his hands in his pockets and started to whistle instead, except he couldn't whistle a single note.

# Six

"What are you up to?" asked Julie, stopping.

"Me?" said Jake.

"Yes, who else is here?"

Tora giggled.

Jake didn't answer.

"Do you have trouble hearing?" Julie took a step forward and shouted right in his ear, "I asked what you're up to!"

Jake backed away in fright.

Tora giggled, covering her mouth with her hand.

"Nothing," said Jake quickly.

"Wrong," said Julie. "It's bad to lie. Anyway, I just saw you standing with your hands in your pockets trying to whistle."

"Why do you ask, since you know that?" said Jake, losing his temper. Julie always had to act dumb like this. She acted even dumber whenever she was with Tora. They were in his class and lived in Number Thirty-nine.

"I want to know why you were standing with your hands in your pockets whistling."

" 'Cause I don't have anything else to do, see?"

"Then don't stand here doing it. You're blocking the path for Tora and me, right?" said Julie, looking at Tora.

Tora just giggled.

Tora had dumb braids. They were much too thin to be fun to pull. He'd tried and knew that he couldn't get a decent grip on them. Margaret's braids were something else. Now hers were real braids.

"Move," said Julie. "We're going that way."

"You can walk on the grass," Jake replied, standing his ground in the middle of the path.

"On the grass?" Julie was horrified. "Are you crazy? Look, it's all wet there, right?"

"So what?" said Jake, getting angry.

"So what?" mimicked Julie.

She walked right up to him and stamped on his toes.

Jake got really scared. She was taller than he. He hadn't noticed that before.

"Listen, you little shrimp," said Julie. "I'm bigger and stronger and Tora and I need a lot of room to get past. Right, Tora?"

Tora nodded, but didn't giggle.

"Scram. It's two against one. We're stronger, you're almost nothing. Watch out, or we'll beat you up."

"Ha," said Jake. "Just try."

Julie sighed. "That's easy," she said, and hit him in the stomach.

It hurt. Hurt terribly. He leaned over forward. Then Tora joined in. They both hit him. One of them jumped him from behind and he fell over. He got all wet. Water soaked in through his pants.

He covered his face with his arms and stopped hitting back.

"Oh, you're giving up?" said Julie. "You're a sissy, you know that? Imagine losing to girls! Wait till we tell the others!"

Then they went away. The last thing he heard was Tora giggling at something Julie said.

But it wasn't the last. Julie turned and shouted, "And you have such a weird father."

Jake wished he were Karl. Then he would shout at them all the worst bad words he knew.

But because he was Jake, he didn't dare say any words like that.

# Seven

"Why're you lying there?"

Jake looked up.

Sara's head seemed to tower high in the sky.

"No reason," he answered, getting up.

Sara came down from heaven and was just as much taller as she usually was.

"Someone beat you up," she said, looking at his face.

Jake shook his head.

Sara took no notice of that. "Who did it? Just tell me, and I'll get them. No one's allowed to be mean to you without my knowing."

She took out a handkerchief. It was almost clean. She spat on it and started rubbing his face.

"In fact you're bleeding," she said.

Jake tried to wriggle away.

"Stay still," she said angrily, and he stood still.

Sara liked looking after Jake. She was kind of like a mom whenever he had a bad time, but, still, no one had given him as many lickings as Sara.

She was ten and not easy to get along with. Lots of kids on the street had found that out. Even Karl, who was just a year younger than she, was scared of Sara, although she was his sister.

"Who did it?" she asked again.

Jake didn't answer.

She shook his arm. "If you don't say, I'll throw you back down on the ground so you'll break your arm."

He knew she'd do it.

"Julie and Tora," he whispered.

"Tora?" Sara sounded as if she couldn't believe that. "I bet it was mostly Julie. Come on, let's go find them."

"No," said Jake. "I don't want to. I'll only get beaten up later."

"I'll look after you," said Sara.

"But Julie has a brother in seventh grade," said Jake.

"But we know Kris, he's in seventh grade too."

"But Kris and Julie's brother are friends, so Kris'll side with Julie and her brother, and we're the ones who'll get licked in the end," said Jake.

Sara thought about that. Then she sighed. "We'll wait and see, for a while at least, till we can decide what to do. We'll get your revenge some time," she said. "We won't put up with things like this."

She put her handkerchief back in her pocket.

"You've got to hit back," she said.

"But there were two of them," Jake answered.

"Tora doesn't count. She just joins in when Julie tells her to."

Jake started to walk off toward the street.

"Where're you going?" said Sara.

"To look for my da . . . father," answered Jake.

"Oh, so he's off again now?" said Sara.

Off again now.

Jake turned back furiously. That was none of her business. Besides, she didn't have to say the nasty, ugly truth of it so clearly.

"It's none of your business," he said hotly.

"Nope," replied Sara. "I didn't say it was. I just asked if— "

"Yeah, I heard what you asked, and you don't need to ask about it!"

Sara looked at him threateningly. "Watch out, or I'll be like Julie!"

Jake clammed up.

Sara would never be like Julie. She'd be much worse. Sara could just turn into being like Sara. And that was the worst a kid on the street could come up against, aside from being tormented by the older boys.

"I'm looking for Karl," said Sara. "Have you seen him?" Jake shook his head.

"Well," said Sara, "I have to look for him. He's probably hiding somewhere in the park. Mom was furious, 'cause he pinched her cigarettes, and they were the last ones she had. If I see your dad, I'll say hi and tell him you're looking for him."

# Eight

Then he caught sight of her.

She was standing still on the sidewalk. Standing quite straight. Not moving, as if someone had bewitched her.

Her blond hair stuck out from under a knitted cap. No one else was wearing winter hats yet. Her coat looked heavy. No one else was wearing a coat.

She had boots on. They were yellow with white trim, the kind boys wore in his class.

Jake looked at her.

She was the nicest person he knew.

She was in 2B. Jake was in 2A. Their classrooms were next to each other.

Every day in school she looked at him at least once. They'd never spoken to each other.

Only looked.

He looked on the sly to see why she was standing like that. She didn't do much of anything, never played with anyone. He'd never seen her with any toys either. Sara left her alone, and that was good.

Mostly she just stood motionless on the sidewalk. Once in a while she would walk slowly over into the park. If she went too far, a window would open in Number Thirty-seven and a woman would stick her head out.

The woman wouldn't say anything, but the girl would hurry back to the sidewalk, and just stand there again.

And her name was Mai Britt.

That was the neatest name Jake had ever heard.

# Nine

Jake was sitting in the living room when Mom got home.

"Hello!" she called from the front hall. "Is anyone home?"

She was always happy when she got back from work even though she was tired and worn out.

Jake went out to her.

"Hi," said Mom. "It's *so* nice you're home."

The way Mom said that, he just had to go over and give her a hug.

She hung up her coat with a sigh.

"There was so much to do today," she said.

That was what she said almost every day, but he could hear from her sigh whether there had been a little more or much much more to do.

"People are never satisfied. They don't know which dress to buy. Is the blue one with white stripes prettier than the yellow one with white flowers? So then they leave without buying anything because they can't make up their minds which dress they like best. Meanwhile I have to hang up all the dresses they've tried on. It's terrible, let me tell you."

They went into the living room.

The smile vanished from Mom's face when she saw the vacuum cleaner standing in the middle of the floor.

She put her arms across her chest when she saw the dirty dishes, still just as many as there had been in the morning.

She sighed when she peered into the bedroom and smelled the bad air and saw the darkness in there.

"Where is he?" she said, and her voice was sad.

Jake shrugged. He wished Mom's voice would be different. He wanted so much to be happy, but it was impossible when Daddy was gone and Mom talked like that.

"Was he home when you came back from school?"

Jake shook his head. His voice had deserted him.

"What was he wearing?"

"Clogs and a Windbreaker," whispered Jake.

"Clogs and a Windbreaker?" Mom was startled. "Clogs and a Windbreaker?" She laughed. "What in the world did he mean by that?"

Jake didn't know.

"What do you think it means?" Mom asked, looking at him.

"He could be anywhere," said Jake.

Mom stroked his head, but it was as if she didn't know what she was doing.

"Anywhere," she murmured.

She went over to the window and stood with her back to him.

"I've been out looking for him," said Jake. He wanted to try to make Mom happy.

She lit a cigarette and blew the smoke toward the window.

"Mommy," he said inside himself, but it didn't get out.

He went toward the window and stopped a little distance behind her.

Mom didn't know he was there.

He put out a hand. Her skirt was soft to take hold of.

She glanced swiftly down at him, smiled a little, but he saw that it was a make-believe smile.

The cigarette had gone out, and she dropped it into the ashtray on the windowsill.

"Well," she said, "we sure have extra work today, the two of us. You'll help me, won't you?"

Jake nodded.

And Daddy had promised to do all that work.

"He must have had a bad time today," said Jake.

"Yes," said Mom, "it looks that way. Clogs and a Windbreaker. Where do you think he could be?"

Jake shook his head. "Anywhere," he mumbled.

He was frightened.

Anywhere. It could be anywhere. In the park, by the

harbor, on the fjord, in the woods behind Sun Mountain, or far, far away, so far that he didn't know the place.

And then what? Perhaps Dad was so far away that he couldn't come home again.

"What if," he begun, but his voice gave out.

"What if what?" said Mom, who had started the vacuum cleaner.

"What if he's so far away that he can't come home again?"

Mom turned off the vacuum cleaner and knelt down in front of him. Then she was shorter than he. Mom was like a little girl, but her eyes were serious.

Mom was kind and nice. She was even nicer than Mai Britt, especially when she was serious or felt sorry.

She took his hands, which got lost in her big hands.

"Jake," she said. "I'm sorry it's like this."

He didn't really understand what she meant.

She stood up again and started the vacuum cleaner.

"I'll straighten up the bedroom," he said.

"Fine," said Mom, and she smiled. This time it was a real smile.

# Ten

Afterward there was nothing to do but wait.

Each sitting in a chair waiting.

Mom had phoned Willy and Jan to say they'd better not come that evening, but what about Saturday? So they decided on Saturday instead.

Mom and Jake were tired. Housecleaning was hard work, especially for Mom, who was worn out when she got back from work.

It had become dark outside. Pale lights peeked out between branches in the park. The lights came from houses on the other side. Kids he didn't know lived over there. He'd seen them in the park and sometimes they took over the playground even though they had one of their own. The kids across the park were dangerous.

Mom and Jake made fried eggs for supper. Mom wasn't up to cooking anything else.

The room was absolutely silent.

Car noises on the street sounded loud. It was almost, Jake thought, as if the cars drove right over the house.

Someone was walking back and forth in the apartment above them. They rarely heard noises from up there.

A tap in the kitchen was dripping. Jake paid no attention to it.

It was awful waiting. Grim.

Sometimes it's nice and fun to wait, like when it's Christmas or your birthday or when you know that Mom or Dad are definitely going to come home in about an hour with a surprise.

That's a great kind of waiting.

But it's awful to sit, each person in a separate chair, not speaking. Just sitting there scared. Thinking about Dad who went out in his clogs and Windbreaker, who might be anywhere.

Jake thought about Sara, who might still be looking for Karl. Just think, Karl was gone too. He could be absolutely anywhere too, of course. But Sara hadn't been scared.

Now and then Jake looked at Mom. She was staring right in front of her, but then her eyelids drooped as if she were falling asleep. Then she would give a start and open her eyes. Every time she looked at Jake, he quickly looked down.

Jake hurt inside. He often felt like that before he began to cry.

He pulled his legs up under him onto the chair. His feet were freezing, but that was because he was anxious. His toes were frightened.

Time drags when you wait. Jake felt he'd been sitting there for hours, but the clock in the bookcase showed that he'd been sitting there only twenty minutes. Strange. He was sure that hours had passed.

He had some toys, of course, but he wasn't up to playing with them. How could he play when Dad might be anywhere at all?

He couldn't do anything but wait.

# Eleven

Suddenly Mom was standing over him, shaking his shoulder.

"Jake," she said quietly, "why don't you go to bed? You're just sleeping in your chair."

And he was. He was tired, he could feel that now.

"What about Daddy?" he began.

"I'm sure you'll hear when he comes home. If you don't, I promise to wake you."

"Really and truly?"

"Word of honor," Mom answered solemnly.

When he got up from the chair, he knew how tired he was. He staggered over to the door.

"Shall I help you?" Mom asked.

"No, I can do it myself," he answered.

He did, but he couldn't quite manage to brush his teeth. Mom usually asked him if he'd done that, but tonight she'd probably let that go, he thought.

He couldn't find his pajamas, so he lay down in his underwear.

But before he lay down, he looked under the bed. No one was there. No one was ever there. But you never know, said Sara. In fact, she knew about someone who had found a whole gang of thieves under his bed.

Then he went over to the closet. No matter how tired he was, he had to do these things every night.

He listened carefully at the closet door. Everything was quiet in there. Carefully he turned the key and pulled it out fast.

A faint noise reached him that instant. The night birds were stirring, but luckily he'd locked them in.

He put the key on the bedside table so he'd be able to grab it easily. He got down on the floor and looked around under the bed one more time because someone just might have hidden in the blackest shadows way back under the bed.

But there was no one there. He'd almost known that definitely, but all the same, he did it to make sure. There'd been times he'd been so scared to look that he'd had to get Mom or Dad to look for him.

He got into the unmade bed.

The door to the hall was not quite closed. He turned off the lamp on the bedside table. Yellow light slipped in to him through the little open space by the door. It felt safe.

He waited for Mom. She always came in to say good night.

He had to wait a long time. Finally the door opened wider and she came in.

"Are you asleep?" she whispered.

"No, I'm awake," he whispered back. "I thought you weren't coming."

Mom sat down on the edge of his bed and stroked his forehead. "Of course I'd come."

"Mom," Jake began, "Dad has never been away so—so long before, has he?"

"Yes, he has. You mustn't worry so. Of course he'll come back."

"But he could be anywhere."

"Is anywhere a dangerous place?"

"Yes."

"I don't think he'll take chances. After all, he's going to start teaching again in a few weeks."

"Is he?" Jake was not sure.

Mom was silent.

"Mom, do you think so?"

"I hope so," Mom answered.

"But what if his nerves don't get well?"

"Yes, Jake, what if," she whispered. "What if."

Mom said that in such a way that he began to freeze.

"We just have to see how it goes."

"Why did he get like this? So weird, I mean. It's

awful. Julie teases me about it, and Karlsen thinks it's peculiar that Daddy is home all day."

Mom sighed. "You mustn't mind what other people think or feel. Why did Dad's nerves get like this? So many reasons really. I don't think he should have become a teacher, at least not in junior high. I tried to tell him that while he was studying. I tried to say it wasn't right for him, but he just got offended and wouldn't listen to me."

"But Mom, what if his nerves don't get well and he just goes on running and running every day. Then what'll we do?"

"I don't think I could take that, Jake. That would be too much for me. I really want to do something else, you know, not work in a dress shop. I was just going to wait until Dad got going in his work."

"Then what would you do?"

"Go back to school. You know I really wanted to teach little kids, but then you started to come and I had to stop. I do want to take the exam, and Dad has no right to ruin it."

She said the last bit in a low voice but it whispered and hurt in his ears.

Then Mom smiled and said, "But we mustn't sit here making things worse than they are. Dad will come home soon, you'll see. And he'll start back in school again too. Things will work out."

Mom patted him on the head and stood up. "I'll wake you when he comes."

Then she went out, leaving the door slightly open after her.

First Mom talked about things as if they were difficult.

Then she talked about them as if everything was going to be all right.

But she didn't think that. Jake knew she said it to comfort him. He could still hear that in her voice.


# Twelve

He couldn't get to sleep. He was sure he couldn't. All night he'd be lying awake waiting. He wouldn't doze off either. Perhaps he should hold his breath as well. Would Dad come home if he did that?

He curled up in his bed.

Anywhere.

That sounded so cold and lonely.

Like autumn wind and nightfall and rain against windowpanes.

That was Dad now with his clogs and his Windbreaker.

# Thirteen

The night birds.

He remembered the first time they were there.

But in a way they'd been there as long as he could remember.

Suddenly one night he'd woken up. Something had woken him.

Dark in the room. Dark in the hall. That was wrong. His door had been left open earlier so that some light would reach him from the hall.

Then he heard them. Buzzing in the air from all sides.

He saw them too. Like black shadows, even blacker than the night. They popped out of the dark and just were there.

Big, flapping wings with feathers that made a rushing sound.

Red, staring eyes. As if they had fire in them.

And beaks—they were open, big, and dangerous. They wanted to peck at him.

Closer and closer, thousands of them. The night was full of birds. The darkness was nothing but birds. His room was bursting with birds.

They wanted to get him.

He screamed and got under the quilt. The first birds struck the bed with their claws and tried to pull off his quilt. He heard the birds scream, loud and shrill. Louder than he could.

He cried and shouted.

Suddenly Mom was there. And Dad.

"Jake!" Mom called from far away.

The quilt was lifted off of him. Lights went on in the room. In the next second he was hiding in Mom's arms. And the birds had gone. Not one feather was left behind.

Jake gasped and sobbed and told what had happened.

Mom stroked his hair and said, "There, there."

Dad looked all around the room but didn't find a single bird.

"Look, the window's closed," he said. "They couldn't get in here. That's the only place they could've come from."

But Jake knew where they came from.

The door to the closet had swung open, and he could see clothes and darkness.

The closet was very deep. Mom and Dad's clothes and his own hung in there, and still there was plenty of space left over.

"They—they came—from the closet," he sobbed. "Look, the door's open. It's the birds that opened it."

"I'm sure we just forgot to close the door properly," said Mom.

"No, it's the birds," said Jake. "I know it's the birds. The door was closed when I went to bed. I know that."

Dad went into the closet and looked around. "Well, anyway they're gone now," he said. "I can't find a single trace of them."

"They're just hiding from you," said Jake. "They're invisible in the light. They'll come back here again as soon as it's dark. If there'd been a light in the hall, they wouldn't have come."

"That was dumb of me," said Dad. "I must have turned it off. I forgot. I'm sorry."

Mom went into the kitchen. Jake heard her opening some drawers.

Then she came back with a key.

"Look here," she said, handing it to him. "This is the key to the closet. Now you can lock the door every night before you go to bed, and then the birds won't come out. Try locking it, and you'll see."

Jake did it. He was not afraid of the closet now that the lights were on in the room and Mom and Dad were there.

The key fit the lock and it was absolutely impossible to open the door after he'd turned the key.

"And I've got something else too," said Mom, going out again.

Soon after she came back with a long string and a little yellow bell with a nice clear ring.

She tied the bell tight to one end of the string.

"I'll hang this bell over our bed," said Mom. "And tomorrow we can fit eyelet screws to the walls here, in the hall and in our bedroom and we can put the string through them. Then if you wake in the night and feel scared, you can pull the end of the string that we'll hang over your bed. Then we'll wake up and one of us can come running into your room right away. Doesn't that sound good?"

"Yes, it does," Jake thought.

Mom hung the bell over the bed as she had said, but the string had to lie along the floor until the next day. She tied the end of the string to his night table.

"Now try it," she said.

Jake had to pull a lot of string toward him before the bell rang in Mom and Dad's room.

"Now it's not dangerous anymore, is it?" Dad asked.

No, now he wasn't scared. But they had to sit with him until he fell asleep, and the light had to be on in the hall.

Since then he'd only seen the birds once, and that was when he'd forgotten to lock the closet door.

But he often heard them. Almost every night, if he listened carefully, which he always did.

Faint wingflaps behind the locked door. As if they sat

waiting, hoping he would forget to lock it. But he didn't forget again.

Tonight the birds were particularly restless. They scratched their claws against the door.

That was probably because Dad was anywhere.

But luckily Mom was sitting in the living room right nearby, so he wasn't scared.

Just the same, he checked to see the key to the closet on his night table.

Anyway, he wasn't very frightened.

Just a little—as long as he didn't think about it too much.


# Fourteen

A key in the lock.

It was Dad who'd come home.

Now Jake felt happy. He didn't know whether he'd been asleep. He heard Mom go out of the living room. He saw Mom pass like a shadow by the opening of his door.

"Erik," she whispered, and then there was only silence.

Jake knew they were standing with their arms around each other, kissing, not speaking.

"I've been so frightened," Mom said a little louder.

Dad didn't answer.

"Why were you so long? What happened?"

"I'm sorry, Linda, I didn't mean to . . ." Dad didn't say any more. His voice showed he was sorry.

Dad went on, "I just had to get out, all of a sudden, and I've been walking and walking. . . ."

"Erik," Mom whispered, but Jake heard she was crying. "Why did you have to do that just now when you're about to start teaching again? You could have phoned at least."

"Yes," replied Dad. "I could've. I'm sorry, I mean it. Really sorry."

There was silence again.

"Jake?" Mom stood in the doorway.

He moved, so they'd know he was awake.

"Erik, go in and see Jake. I promised to wake him when you got home. He probably hasn't been able to sleep yet, poor guy. He was so worried about you that he went out looking for you."

Dad came in. He was still wearing his Windbreaker.

He sat on the edge of the bed.

"Jake?" His voice was low. His hand was warm.

"Forgive me for not being home," said Dad, "but I had to get out. I don't really know why, it was as if the walls were trying to suffocate me. So I had to get out."

"Yes," said Jake, "I knew something had happened. But how can walls suffocate you, Daddy?"

39

"That was only what I felt," he answered. "It was my nerves again."

So it was his nerves again. Jake was worried.

"But you know you're starting at school again soon, and then no one should notice your nerves," he said.

"That's right, Jake, then they shouldn't show," said Dad, "but it's just so hard to hide them. I can't just snap my fingers and say shazam and they're gone. It won't work, Jake."

No, that really wouldn't work at all.

It was good that Dad was home again. He put his hand on Dad's hand and pressed it against his cheek.

"Where have you been?" he asked.

"Walking around," said Dad. "I tried to go see Fritz, but he wasn't home."

"Where did you go?" asked Jake.

"Well," answered Dad, "nowhere in particular."

"Was that far?"

"That depends," said Dad. "Tonight it wasn't far."

"Is it so far it might be impossible to come back?"

"But I did come back," said Dad. "I suppose it could be so far a person couldn't come back."

"Are you going to go that far someday?" There was fear in Jake's voice.

"I hope not, Jake. I'll always try to turn back before I get that far."

"I was out looking for you."

Dad stroked his cheek.

"But I didn't know where to look because you were wearing clogs and your Windbreaker. You don't usually wear them together."

"No," said Dad. "I forgot to put something else on my feet. But I'm back now."

"Yes," said Jake. "You're back again."

"Can you sleep?"

"I think so. How late is it?"

"It's after twelve. Much too late for you, right?"

Yes, that was true, and he had to be in school at nine the next morning.

"Shall I sit here until you're asleep?"

"You could sit in the living room with Mom."

It was nice to lie waiting for sleep when he could hear their voices in the living room, and the light was on in the hall.

Dad got up.

"Are the birds quiet?" he asked.

"They will be now," Jake answered.

"Then good night, Jake," said Dad.

"Good night, Daddy," said Jake, feeling happy once more.

But deep inside he had a little sore spot. It was always there.

# Fifteen

"Jake, Jake!"

Someone was shaking him.

"Wake up. You have to go to school!"

He opened his eyes. Right now? He'd just gotten to sleep. Mom was standing by the bed. "Jake! You have to get up!"

She smiled at him.

"It's eight o'clock, and I have to run, you know. If you hurry, you'll have time to eat breakfast with Dad before you have to be in school."

"Mmm," mumbled Jake.

Mom pulled open the curtains. Outside was a blue autumn sky and a yellow September sun.

"It's nice out today," said Mom. "Have a good time, Jake, and look after Dad so he doesn't disappear."

She smiled when she said that, but her voice was serious.

She really meant it in a way.

Look after Dad.

The front door closed. Mom was rushing to the dress shop to sell clothes to customers who couldn't make up their minds.

Jake didn't want to get up. He was tired. He hadn't done his lessons.

Dad stood in the doorway. He was wearing the white, thick turtleneck sweater and blue corduroy pants. Dad's casual clothes. He wore them when he felt good about himself.

He had smile lines around his eyes as he stood there looking at Jake.

Dad was nice-looking. Medium-long blond hair that was always shiny. A short beard that grew close to his face, just as blond as his hair. It tickled when Dad gave him hugs.

Mom said that Dad hid behind his beard.

"Could be," Dad had answered.

"Hi," said Dad. "Are you going to get up?"

"I don't know," replied Jake.

"Are you sick?"

"I don't know."

Dad was concerned.

"I was so worried about you," said Jake. "It's so bad when you just go off like that."

"I'm sorry about it," said Dad.

They looked at each other, and Jake knew that he had gotten out of going to school that day.

"You're not really well," said Dad.

Actually he was fine, but he didn't feel too well if he had to go to school.

"I feel bad," he said.

"Where?" Dad asked, seriously again.

"I should have done my homework," answered Jake. Dad didn't laugh.

"You must be tired and a little groggy today," he said.

Jake nodded.

"I think you'd better stay home," said Dad. "After all, it's my fault you haven't done your lessons and are tired."

Jake nodded again. What Dad said was true.

"But if you feel like getting up, we can have a nice long breakfast. Afterward we can go out into the world and see what we can find."

Jake felt up to that.

It was all he felt up to today.

# Sixteen

Dad drank his coffee and looked out the window.

Jake ate bread and cheese and drank some milk.

The radio announcer said it was nine o'clock.

Now school had started. Everyone was there, except perhaps Olaf, because he'd been sick several days.

Now everyone must be thinking Jake was sick too.

In a way he had been. Dad understood that.

Mom would eventually understand too, he hoped.

Dad sat not saying anything.

Jake thought about yesterday. He pictured in his mind the vacuum cleaner, the dirty dishes, and the messy bedroom.

"Daddy!" he said.

Dad looked at him over the coffee cup he was holding with both hands.

"Where did you go yesterday?"

Dad just looked at him. His eyes looked large over the edge of the cup.

"I tried to walk away from my sadness," he answered.

"Why are you so sad?" asked Jake.

Dad put down the coffee cup and propped up his head with both hands.

"Nothing works out for me," he answered. "Everything I do goes wrong."

"But then can't you do right things?" Jake was surprised that it wasn't possible.

"I try to, Jake, but it goes wrong."

"So then is it wrong for you to be in the school?"

Dad gave a little nod. "Yes," he said, "I think so. I'm frightened of the kids, you see."

"Mom said you shouldn't be a teacher," said Jake.

"Yes, she said that when I started studying, but I didn't listen to her. Didn't want to listen. I'd decided to become a teacher, and I was determined. I had tried it out a while as a substitute. It wasn't as good as I'd thought, but I was sure it would get better once I'd studied. But Mom was right."

"Tommy's Dad works for the railroad, and Tora's Dad is a taxi driver."

Dad started spinning the cup around in the saucer.

"Actually, I've had several jobs, but I didn't really like any of them. After graduation I was in a bookstore for a while, because I didn't know what I wanted to do. But that got to be so hard, I felt there were too many people. Then I got a job in an office. But there was too much paperwork and just sitting. And I still didn't know what I really felt I wanted to do."

Jake sat listening. Dad was talking to him as if he were grown up and understood everything he said.

"So then I met Mom, you know. She wanted to teach in lower school. We were so young, both of us. She was eighteen and I was one year older. Then Mom had only just started in teacher's training school when she found out that she was going to have a baby, and that was you. So she stopped, we got married, and I went on at that terrible office."

Dad sighed. Jake said nothing, just listened.

"We agreed that I'd work a couple of years while Mom was home with you, and then she'd start school again so she could get the training to be what she wanted to be. I managed to change jobs but only landed in another office where there was even more paperwork, and lots of noise. Mom was happy about

46

her plans, she knew what she wanted, and she sounded so enthusiastic that I felt like trying something like it myself. So then I applied to teacher's college, and got in. By then you were all of four, and Mom had a half-day job. She hadn't started school again, unfortunately. When I was accepted by the school and terribly much wanted to go there, Mom said she could work full time for the three years I'd be in school. Then afterward, when I started teaching, she intended to make something of herself. She never did think all that time that I was cut out to be a teacher, but she certainly hoped I'd find it out myself."

"Did you?" asked Jake.

"Yes," answered Dad, "I did, but didn't want to admit it. I wanted to go through with it. And see—what came of it. Nothing. And Mom was supposed to start school this fall. But I ran away from my job after three days. Now what'll I do, Jake?"

Dad got up and put the coffee cup on the counter.

No, Jake didn't know. But he understood that in any case everything was difficult for Dad.

"Now let's go out," said Dad suddenly. "I don't want to sit here any longer thinking about myself and my nerves. We'll go up on Sun Mountain and see to the end of the world."

"Can we see that far?" asked Jake.

"If you want to," replied Dad.

Jake felt a little troubled.

47

"The laundry," he said. "You're supposed to wash clothes today."

Dad looked at him and smiled. "First we'll go up the mountain and see to the end of the world. After that we'll come home and wash clothes and tidy up the place. We must do the most important things first."

Jake remembered how Mom had looked yesterday when she saw the mess at home. She was disappointed and a little angry.

"The laundry is the most important," said Jake. "We can go up the mountain afterward."

Dad laughed. "That's our dull part," he said. "No, we should go up the mountain first. When the sun gets higher in the sky, we won't be able to see to the end of the world. We have to do it now before it's too late. Then afterward we'll hurry home and wash clothes and make the house shiny-clean like in an ad."

Dad was already out in the hall. "Come on!"

## Seventeen

It was strange to be outside when he really should have been in school.

He'd never cut school before. He knew perfectly well

that that was what he was doing. Last night he'd been sick, not the kind of sickness that means you really can stay home from school, but still—

It was strange to walk down the street. He felt that everyone was watching him go by as if they were trying to figure out why he wasn't in school.

He held on to his dad's hand hard.

Finally he had to ask, "Dad, is everyone looking at me?"

"Looking at you?" said Dad in surprise. "Why should they?"

"To figure out whether . . . whether . . . I'm sick," said Jake in a low voice.

Dad looked down at him. "No," he answered, "no one is looking at you."

But Jake wasn't sure.

At the bus stop he tried to hide behind Dad, because farther up in the line was Julie's mom, and he was almost certain that she knew who he was. But he thought she hadn't caught sight of him.

When he and Dad got in and sat some way behind her, she was so busy talking to a lady sitting next to her that she didn't notice them.

Not until he sat down by the window did Jake let out his breath easily.

Sun Mountain was the end of the line.

Only Dad and Jake were on the bus when it stopped there.

Sun Mountain was not really its name. Mom and Dad had thought up that name. Jake liked it. It was good to think about a place where there was always sun, even though he knew it might be rainy or foggy up there as well.

Sun Mountain was not a real mountain. It was a gently sloping hill with a road going over it, but there was a fantastic view from the top.

On three sides they could see to the far horizon. Behind them a restaurant had been built that blocked the view behind it, but they couldn't see far that way in any case, because real mountains rose farther back there, closing off the view.

There were park benches along the road from which to look at the view, and little tables and trash cans.

Below them spread the town. It was quite a way down. The town was almost nothing but roofs and streets and little black cars moving around fast.

It was windy and Jake felt cold. He really should have brought along a scarf, but no one had started wearing scarves yet.

Dad had put his fishing jacket on over the pullover and he had his hands in his pockets.

They were standing way up close to the railing where the edge of the mountain dropped right down to the edge of the woods far below them. This was the only place on the mountain where they got a sick feeling in their stomachs from looking down. Besides that, they could also see the slope of the mountain, which didn't look so terribly steep.

The wind was ruffling Dad's hair as if it wanted to make it fly away. That was fun to see. Dad didn't pay any attention, just let the wind carry on.

"Look," he said, pointing.

"At what?" said Jake.

"Our town."

"Yes," said Jake.

"We're standing here like giants, looking out over a tiny toy town," said Dad. "Isn't it strange to see the whole town all at once?"

Yes, Jake thought so too. When he was back home on the street, all he saw was the street, the nearest house, the park, and a little of the yards across the way, but now he saw everything. He and Dad had been here several times before, alone and together with Mom. It was just as amazing to see the town every time.

He had never heard before that they could see to the end of the world.

"Where's the end of the world, Dad?" asked Jake.

Dad squinted his eyes as he peered out over the fjord. He didn't say anything. He just looked.

"Do you see the little white clouds far off in the sky, the ones over that low mountain ridge you can just make out dimly, rising from the sea?"

Jake nodded. He saw the clouds. They lay absolutely still as if they were sleeping.

"Can you see that something's shining behind the clouds? A tiny little bit. It's as if the sun is shining on something or other there."

Jake looked. He looked more closely. He climbed up on the fence. Dad held him around his waist so he wouldn't fall. He had to lift him up even further, but even so he didn't see anything glittering, as if the sun were shining on something behind the clouds.

"I don't see anything," he said, disappointed.

"Don't you?" said Dad, holding him close.

Jake shook his head.

"It's glittering really nicely," said Dad. "Faintly, almost as if it isn't there, but still it is."

"Is that the end of the world?" asked Jake.

Dad nodded slowly. "Yes," he answered softly. "I'd really like to think it was."

"Why can't I see it?" Jake didn't understand.

"Perhaps because you don't know what to look for," answered Dad, putting him down.

"Come on," he said suddenly, before Jake could ask what he meant. "Let's run over to the restaurant and have a soda and a pastry. Want to?"

Did he ever!

It certainly was cold, but he felt that a soda and a pastry would warm him up.

# Eighteen

They sat next to a window that was full of blue sky. The tablecloth was white, with interesting spots.

Jake had drunk up his soda and he only just had room for the pastry. He wouldn't have eaten breakfast if he'd known about this.

Jake felt they'd sat there a long time and he started to get restless. It didn't look as if Dad was thinking about going home. His smile had come back. He wasn't sad the way he'd been while they had breakfast, when he talked about the school.

"Aren't we having a good time!" said Dad all at once, as if he realized that Jake was thinking about something sad.

Jake nodded. "Yes," he answered, "but Mom should've come along."

Dad glanced swiftly at the clock. "The laundry," he said.

Then he stole a look at Jake and laughed. "You sly fox," he said. "I get your message. But you're right, it would have been more fun if Mom were with us."

They took the next bus back to town. Dad and he were the only ones to sit in it from Sun Mountain, but gradually more and more people got on. When they came to the center of town, the bus was completely full, and lots of people were standing.

They raced from the bus stop across to the sidewalk. There was almost no one in sight at the moment, but suddenly Dad stopped.

"Jake," he said, "come, let's cross over to the other side of the street."

Jake had stopped a little way in front of Dad. "Why should we? We live on this side."

"Yes, but can't we cross over?" he said, taking Jake's hand.

Jake didn't understand why he was being dragged over to the other sidewalk along the park. They should be going home to do the laundry, and they only had a block to go.

But then he understood. Over on the sidewalk where they'd just been, Karlsen and Lie were walking toward them.

Lie was the chairman of the sportsclub in the street; he'd tried to convince Dad several times to join and play table tennis or handball or something else, but Dad said no.

Lie didn't understand why, because all the other fathers did some kind of sports activity.

"He gives me a strange look when I meet him," Dad would say. "As if there were something wrong with me because I don't want to play table tennis."

And Karlsen. He thought it was really crazy that Dad was home while his wife was out working. Jake had heard Karlsen say this to Mom once, and Dad had obviously found out about it. In any case he tried to avoid those two whenever he caught sight of them.

"I'm scared of them," Dad told Mom once. "They watch me."

Jake had heard that.

Dad regretted what he'd said, once they were safe in the apartment.

"Dad," said Jake anxiously, "come on, let's hurry with the laundry and get everything done by the time Mom comes home."

# Nineteen

"Hello!" said Mom. "Is anyone home?"

"Yes," called out Dad and Jake at the same time from the kitchen.

Mom looked in on them. "How good it smells!" she said. "What is it?"

"Dad's special meat loaf," said Jake. "Did you see the laundry on the line down in the yard? I hope you noticed they're our clothes."

Mom laughed. "Yes, I saw them."

Jake had set the table. It felt strange putting a knife and fork to the side of each plate, so he put them above the plates instead.

Mom was cheerful now because Dad was home and had done something.

Dad was good at doing things when he didn't run off.

The meal was good.

Mom said she'd never tasted such a good meat loaf.

Then she asked of course how the day had gone in school.

Jake looked swiftly at Dad. Dad looked at Mom.

"Jake didn't go to school today. He was a little under the weather this morning as you can imagine."

Mom looked from one to the other of them.

Then she said, "Oh yes, I didn't notice that this morning because I was so rushed."

Luckily Mom wasn't angry.

"Did you go see Fritz today?" Mom asked.

"Fritz?" he said, surprised. "No, why should I go to the doctor today?"

"I did get the impression that you'd tried to talk with him yesterday afternoon."

"Oh, then, yes," said Dad, as if that had been a million years ago.

Mom got up and came back with her handbag.

"Here," she said, taking out a pill bottle, which she put next to Dad's plate.

"What's that?" he said.

"Pills from Fritz. I thought you probably hadn't been there today, so I phoned and spoke to him. He wants you to go have a talk with him."

Dad looked at the pills. He looked at Mom. He was stern. Then he turned sad. Then he got angry. Jake saw him clench his teeth.

"Pills," he pressed the word out through his lips. "So pills are going to make me well, are they?"

"Erik," said Mom despairingly, "you know that's not what they're for."

"Then what're they for?"

"They'll just help you if you suddenly get depressed and low. They won't make you well. Fritz wants you to go talk with him. He said you hadn't been there in a long time."

Dad's voice trembled. "You two are always doing something behind my back."

Jake looked at Dad. It was terrible when he talked like that. It was like hearing little kids on the street when they were mad at their moms.

"Erik," Mom put her hand on his shoulder.

Dad suddenly stood up and walked out of the room. He closed the door to the bedroom quietly behind him.

Mom and Jake looked at each other.

Jake was frightened again.

"Did you two have a good time today?" Mom asked in a tired voice.

Jake nodded.

"Would you like some more food?" Mom asked.

He shook his head and left the table.

"I'm going outside for a while," he said.

He had to after this.

"Sure, go ahead," replied Mom, starting to clear the table. But then she immediately sat down again and stared blankly straight in front of her.

"Take care," said Jake, looking back in at her quickly.

Mom gave him a brief smile.

It was good to get out on the street.


# Twenty

Naturally he met Julie right away. Without Tora.

"Why weren't you in school today?" she asked sharply.

"Because I was sick, right?" he answered.

"Oh, really," she said angrily. "And now you're well again."

"Yes, imagine that," said Jake.

"Don't you know you're not allowed to go out on a day you're absent from school?" she said.

"No, imagine that," said Jake. "It's not true."

"Yes, imagine that," said Julie, stepping on his toes. It was strange he hadn't noticed long ago that she was taller than he, considering she stood on his toes so often.

"Besides, my mom saw you on the bus today, you see."

Jake didn't know what to answer.

"Know what I think?" said Julie.

"No," replied Jake, although he really did know.

"I think you played hooky today. You just wait, I'll tell the teacher you played hooky. Then you'll get it, I bet."

She tossed her head and walked away from him.

Dumb Julie with that dumb mom of hers!

Now he couldn't go to school tomorrow either.

# Twenty-one

He found Karl in the park.

He was sitting almost out of sight under the bushes by the big oak tree.

Jake wouldn't have found him if he hadn't known that he usually sat there.

Karl was smoking. He didn't hide the cigarettes the moment he saw someone coming.

"It's you," was all he said, blowing smoke right in Jake's face. Jake coughed. Karl laughed. Jake got angry.

"You stole those cigarettes," he said.

"I sure did," replied Karl, "but only from my mom, so it doesn't count."

"Besides, you're not allowed to smoke," said Jake. "You're not old enough."

"Older than you anyway, crybaby," replied Karl, blowing more smoke at him.

"But I don't smoke," returned Jake.

"That's 'cause you're a cowardly drip," said Karl, sending up a smoke ring that hung on a branch.

Jake was impressed. He hadn't known that Karl could blow smoke rings.

"Drip yourself," he said.

Karl blew a storm into his face. Jake coughed, and tears came. The worst was that Karl laughed.

"I can leave, and I will," coughed Jake.

He turned to go.

"Now don't be a dumb drip," said Karl. "A little smoke won't ruin your small, childish lungs. I won't do it anymore."

Jake came back and sat down next to him.

It was exciting to be with Karl.

It was dangerous to be with Karl.

He did so many crazy things, and he was the worst tough kid on the whole street. That's what adults said, but they also said it was because he came from such a difficult home. Jake had been to his home once but he didn't see what could be so difficult about it.

"Want a smoke?" asked Karl, offering him a crumpled pack of cigarettes.

Jake shook his head.

It was great that Karl asked him, Jake thought, because that meant Karl didn't think of him only as a crybaby.

It was even better that Karl didn't get mean when he refused. That was really great.

"Sara was looking for you yesterday," said Jake. He felt like knowing where Karl had been.

"I know," replied Karl, rubbing his hands on his pant legs.

The remarkable thing about Karl was, whatever he wore, he got filthy dirty the minute he went out. Jake got dirty too, but never as bad as Karl. Jake didn't understand how he did it.

"I sat here and heard Sara calling me, but I didn't say a word."

"Why not?" asked Jake.

"She had a good time walking around looking for a while," he answered.

"I bet you got a hiding from her when you finally went home."

"Don't bet on it," answered Karl.

"I know you did," said Jake. "Sara's stronger than you."

"Shut up, none of your business," said Karl.

Then Jake was sure that Karl had got a hiding. Sara enjoyed beating up other people. It was one of the few things she liked.

Jake hadn't meant to tell anyone that he had played hooky that day but he had to tell when he was with Karl. Suddenly it felt important for Karl to know.

"I cut school today," he said, looking out into space, trying to sound as if it were something he was in the habit of doing.

Karl didn't answer. He was stubbing out the cigarette on the damp ground.

"I said I cut school today," Jake said louder, looking at Karl when he said it.

Karl didn't look up. "So what? What's so special about that?" He yawned.

"Nothing." Jake was disappointed that Karl wasn't concerned.

"I cut a lot. Like tomorrow I'll meet one of the big guys and make a deal right during class time."

"What kind of deal?"

"Don't pry, crybaby, it's just for us big guys."

"I'm almost as big as you," said Jake.

"But not as strong," Karl said back, knocking him over with a shove.

Jake wasn't afraid of saying things like that to Karl. Most of the kids on the street were afraid of him, but Karl was never as mean to him as he was to the others.

That was probably because Jake had Sara to look after him.

Jake scrambled up again.

"Where're you going?" he asked.

"Off," answered Karl, spitting in a long arc.

Jake didn't know how to do that.

"Where?" asked Jake.

"Home to my own front stoop," replied Karl. "Want to know anything else?" He stuck his hands in his pockets like some kind of private eye.

Jake walked beside him.

Tommy was waiting across the street. Karl waved to him. They were in the same class.

"So long," said Karl, waving the way that detective would have.

Jake didn't answer. It all happened too fast for him.

He watched Karl run across the street to Tommy. They started walking down the sidewalk.

Suddenly Tommy turned and called out so loud it carried over the noise of the traffic, "Have you found your daddy yet?"

Jake couldn't be bothered to answer.

# Twenty-two

He was alone.

Lights were on in the living room window at home, but he didn't let himself be taken in. It wasn't as cozy up in there as it looked.

There was no one to be with. He wasn't big enough to go along with Karl and Tommy. Or tough enough either.

He missed Roald. They hadn't done all that much together before Roald moved away, but still he missed him.

Jake wished he were Karl lots of times, wished he could say the same things, do the same things. Also, Karl went around with the big boys. They didn't pay any attention to him.

He sighed and turned.

It was getting dark under the trees.

From the playground came the sound of kids shouting. It was almost never any fun there. Too many kids wanted to play with the same few things all the time.

Sometimes Jake wished he were more than one person. Imagine if he could just say: "Now I want three of me to play with." And then there would be three more of him. That would be really great.

Then he wouldn't be enemies with them because they'd be so much like him, and they'd like to play the same games.

But that was one of many impossible things.

What should he do?

He walked a short way into the park.

A girl was coming toward him down a path a short distance away.

It was Tora. She was alone too.

She stopped when she caught sight of him. Then she ran off fast to one side and hurried out onto the sidewalk.

Tora was afraid when she wasn't with Julie.

# Twenty-three

On his way in to his apartment building he met Sara in the entry.

"What were you doing in our courtyard?" he asked, somewhat angrily.

He felt that everybody was doing and saying things they shouldn't be today.

"Didn't you hear it?" whispered Sara with big round eyes.

Jake didn't know anyone whose eyes got as round as Sara's when she was going to tell about something exciting.

"What?"

"The screams, of course," she said irritably.

A lump grew in his stomach. He was scared.

"Screams," he said carefully.

"Yes." Now Sara was whispering. She dragged him along into the entry where it was almost completely dark.

"Some awful screams woke me up last night," she whispered right into his ear. Her breath tickled, but he didn't dare pull away from her.

"I got up and looked out the window, 'cause the screams came from the street. And do you know what I saw?"

"No," whispered Jake. His heart was pounding so hard that he almost didn't hear what Sara said.

"I saw a–a–a huge shadow sneaking along the wall of our house, and do you know what?"

"No," whispered Jake.

"The shadow was dragging something behind it. You know what it was?"

"No," whispered Jake.

"A person."

A chill went up and down Jake's spine. What Sara

66

said couldn't be true. It mustn't be. She said a lot of strange things. But then after all she was old enough to know a good lot more than he did.

"And then?" he whispered.

"I saw the shadow go into your entry," she said.

"Here?" Jake started and glanced out into the courtyard. It was somewhat lighter there than in the entry itself.

Sara nodded. Her hair tickled his cheek. Her glasses bumped against his nose.

"What was the shadow?" whispered Jake.

"A murderer," said Sara. "This morning there was blood along our wall. It's gone now, but it was there this morning."

"A murderer?" Jake's throat was all dry.

Sara nodded. "And he was dragging a person he'd murdered. Now he's in your basement."

"Our basement? How do you know?"

"I saw him peek out the cellar door a little while ago. But when he saw me standing watching him, he hurried back in again."

"But," Jake felt he had to pee because Sara was telling him such terrible things, "but—then why didn't he murder you?"

"Because he was afraid of me, of course," said Sara. "No one dares do anything to me; besides, I wear glasses."

"Oh, right."

Sara was lucky to be strong and have glasses.

"What'll we do about it?" said Jake.

"Do?" Sara was surprised.

"Yes, don't we have to tell the police or someone?"

"Oh, no," said Sara, "we don't. —We'll catch him all by ourselves the minute he sneaks out and doesn't see us. And then we'll get a reward and be in the newspapers and all the murdered people will be able to go home again."

"But they're all dead," said Jake.

"Don't talk so much," said Sara, "or I'll knock you down."

Jake shut up. He knew she could do that as easy as anything.

"But I don't dare live here if there's a murderer in our basement."

Sara humphed. "He won't do anything to you, you know."

How could she be so sure?

"Could you come upstairs with me?" he asked very quietly.

"Are you scared?" said Sara.

Jake nodded. He couldn't deny it, and it didn't matter that he told Sara, because she was brave and liked to protect him.

Sara smiled. "There's no danger when Sara's here to look after you," she said, taking his hand. "I'll go up with you, of course."

They walked out into the courtyard and pushed open the door to his stairway.

There were six steps down to the basement door. They were dark brown and disgusting.

Sara stopped. "Here," she whispered. "This is where I stood and saw the door being opened slowly and a head poke out."

Jake squeezed her hand. "Can't we hurry upstairs?"

"Shouldn't we wait and see whether he comes out again?" said Sara.

"No!" shouted Jake so loud it echoed in the stairwell.

He tugged Sara, who had to run to keep up with him.

Luckily he remembered to jump over the brown spot on the fourth step. Sara also stepped around it.

Sara waited all the time until he'd unlocked his door and was inside his hall. Then she ran off downstairs again to watch the basement door.

Jake sighed.

Now he had one more thing to fear in his house.

# Twenty-four

Mom was lying on the sofa reading a book.

Dad was sitting in the good armchair with his earphones on, listening to records—probably Beethoven, because Dad got nice and melancholy from his music.

Mom smiled at him and put down her book.

"Hi," she said. "I was starting to wonder what had become of you."

Dad waved and smiled at him.

Everything looked as if it was all right. Mom and Dad were definitely friends again.

Dad was special in that he could say, "I'm sorry," and "I didn't mean it."

He often did act very strange when his nerves cracked, he admitted that himself.

"How pale you are!" said Mom. "Are you ill?"

Jake shook his head. "It's nothing," he said.

"Shall I make you some food?" Mom asked.

He was a little hungry when he thought about it, but he was more tired than hungry. He wanted to get into bed right away even though he was sure he couldn't sleep after the terrible things Sara had told him.

But he went to bed anyway after he had looked under the bed and locked the closet and looked under the bed again.

He fixed the door so it was a little more open than usual.

He was allowed to read awhile before going to sleep, but tonight everything was spinning around in his head. He had to put the book aside even though it was a really neat story.

He lay there a long time listening for sounds from the

living room. It was quiet in there. Only now and then did he hear little sounds they made.

But the birds in the wardrobe were restless again and the last thing he heard before he fell asleep was their claws scratching against the closet door.

But they couldn't get out and do anything to him because the door was locked and the key was on the bedside table next to him. As usual.

# Twenty-five

The moment he woke up the next morning he knew there was something he dreaded.

School.

Julie, who'd tell on him.

That jerk Julie with that dumb mom of hers.

Then he remembered Sara and the murderer in the basement, but that didn't matter now. When it was daytime, dangerous things weren't so dangerous any-more. He even wondered whether he should go down into the basement and look around.

Jake woke up before Mom woke him. He heard her trying to be quiet in the bathroom. Then she came out.

"Jake?" she said in the door opening.

"I'm awake," he said.

"Hurry, so we can have breakfast together," she said.

Dad had also gotten up. He was boiling eggs in the kitchen. He smiled at Jake and said, "Hi, good morning."

It was as if yesterday's ghastly things hadn't happened.

Jake thought that was strange. After all, he knew things had happened yesterday that made both Mom and Dad sad, but today they were their ordinary selves again.

They had a cozy breakfast.

"I'll go see Fritz today," said Dad. "I want to talk to him."

"Fine," said Mom.

Otherwise they didn't say very much while they ate. That didn't matter to Jake as long as everything was all right again.

He dreaded school but he didn't dare stay away today as well.

Mom and he were able to walk part of the way together, then they each went in a different direction.

Mom turned four times to wave before she disappeared around the corner.

Jake slowly crossed the street. For his part, if only time would stand still. That would be just fine.

"Jake!" someone called behind him.

Jake didn't turn because he knew who it was. Henrik, snot-nosed and fat, who always hung around him.

Jake put some speed on. He didn't want to walk with Henrik. He didn't like him.

"Hey, Jake, wait up!"

But he didn't wait. He almost ran.

Henrik was really terrible to lend toys and books to; he never returned them. When Jake once in a great while would go over to Henrik's home to get back a toy, he never found it. Henrik's mom always said that she hadn't seen that toy, so Henrik mustn't have it. She said Jake probably hadn't remembered correctly.

Henrik was as fat as his mom and dad.

If only he weren't so snot-nosed. He always was. He sniffed and used the sleeves of his sweater as handkerchiefs, so his sleeves were stiff with snot, especially on the days that he cried a lot because he got beat up. Henrik was beat up a lot because he was fat and sniveling and not at all good at running.

Jake didn't like the way Henrik tried to hang around with him in every free period.

Jake didn't have a lot of friends, but he wasn't lonely enough to want to be with Henrik.

"Jake."

Jake ran.

"Bag of shit!" Henrik shouted after him.

Jake turned in at the school yard and instantly remembered Julie and her mom.

He was filled with dread.

# Twenty-six

Before his first class.

Jake sat looking in his schoolbag. Pretending to look. Henrik walked by without saying a word. He was grumpy and angry. That didn't bother Jake.

Julie came in and positioned herself in front of his seat. She had done up her blond hair in pigtails over her ears.

Jake thought she had ugly ears.

"That car you have," she began.

Jake knew what she meant. He'd been given a photograph of a fantastic antique car with old-fashioned people sitting in it. Willy had given him the picture one time he went over to their house.

The picture was extra-special because it was glossy.

"I want it," said Julie, stretching out her hand.

Jake looked at her. Her eyes were small and mean.

He took out his reader, which was where he kept the picture. He often sat looking at the car during class.

He took out the photo and looked at it for the last time. It was really neat. But he had no choice.

Julie grabbed it out of his hands.

She didn't even say thanks.

Then she went to her place.

"You have ugly ears," he said softly to himself.

But he was somewhat relieved.

Julie wouldn't say anything now.

And he was right. She sat absolutely silent and didn't let on when Jake told the teacher that he'd been sick yesterday.

# Twenty-seven

During the first free period Henrik got beat up. He wouldn't lend the lollipop he was licking. Klaus in the third grade was the one who wanted a lick.

Henrik said, "No no no!"

That didn't help any. Klaus was quicker and stronger. When Henrik tried to run away, Klaus put out his foot so Henrik tripped and fell and dropped the lollipop on the asphalt. Luckily it didn't break, just got dirty.

Klaus refused to take the lollipop until Henrik had licked it clean. Henrik didn't want to. Then Klaus sat on top of him and started hitting him.

The others gathered around to watch and shout.

Jake too. He felt it was unfair of Klaus. Jake felt sorry for Henrik, but did nothing to help him.

Everyone stood there shouting "Get him, Klaus!" not

because they sided with him, but because he was the strongest one there and they were scared of him.

The teacher came running over and lifted Klaus off and asked what it was all about. He didn't get a decent explanation. He was mad at Klaus because he had hit Henrik. And he was mad at Henrik for having a lollipop since they weren't allowed in school.

Jake walked away from them.

Then he saw that Mai Britt was standing over near the fence. She hadn't been watching what was happening.

They looked at each other for a little while. Then lots of kids came between them, and the bell rang for the next class.

# Twenty-eight

During free period after lunch Julie was the one who had a rough time.

She had a fight with Gus and Anita.

All Jake heard was that they were shouting at each other. Julie shouted the loudest. Then she shoved and pushed Gus until he fell and Anita started crying.

Then Susanna, who was Anita's best friend, got mad and said that Julie shouldn't touch decent people with her gross fingers, she who didn't even have a father.

Julie hit her, and Susanna started crying.

Susanna hit her back, and Julie started crying.

Gus had gotten back on his feet again. He was really mad and started shouting while more and more of the others joined in with:

Bright little Julie's shiny nose,

Pull on her pigtails and see how it glows.

Julie yelled at the top of her lungs.

Jake kept a good distance away from there. He didn't want any part of it.

Still, he felt sorry for Julie.

Gus was gross, but he didn't dare say that, because Gus was a good friend of Klaus.

# Twenty-nine

Luckily Roald was in school that day. He was often not there because he was ill.

He was in Mai Britt's class.

Roald and Jake just managed to say a few words that day. It was right before the last class started.

"Hi," said Roald. "Could you come over to my house soon? You haven't come in a while."

Jake was happy. Roald had been just about his best friend before he moved.

Roald didn't want to change schools, so he commuted with his dad to and from school every day even though it was a long way.

"Sure," said Jake, "I will."

Class began.

He was pleased that Roald had talked to him. Sometimes it was as if Roald forgot he was there—he just went around with his own class—but today he'd spoken to him. Jake forgot Julie and Henrik and Klaus for a while.

It was good to think about Roald.

Even though they almost never spent any time together anymore.


# Thirty

It was weird.

Someone was always being mean to someone else.

Even when they played, people almost always became enemies and someone would say someone else cheated.

Everyone got angry at everyone else, and everyone was scared of the ones who were bigger and stronger.

Everyone was frightened of Karl. Jake was too, but not as much as many of the others were.

Jake thought about the ones who were always treated badly.

Henrik was one of those. He certainly had a hard time.

Jake was basically lucky. Of course, the others were mean to him sometimes, but not as often as they were to Henrik and Evie and Ollie.

Jake made a point of keeping together with the strong boys and pretending to be their friend.

He needed to; if not, he'd certainly get more beatings than he did now.

But that wouldn't work for Henrik.

He was sniveling and fat and no good at running. The bigger, stronger boys didn't want him along, because they wanted to be mean to him.

Evie always wore such weird clothes. It was easy to make her cry, so it wasn't surprising that they were mean to her.

She cried in a peculiar way. She yelled as if someone had stuck her with a pin or pinched her, even though whoever was being mean might be standing far away from her.

All anyone had to do was look at her for a long time or say "fatty" even though she was thin, or say "boo" and she'd start yelling and screaming.

The big boys thought that was neat.

Jake didn't feel it was nice, although he did laugh along with the others.

Ollie walked with a limp.

The big boys imitated him. Sometimes they walked in a long line behind him until he'd sit down and cry.

Ollie was in third grade, but looked as if he were in the first, and he cried a lot. So it wasn't strange that people were mean to him.

Jake had also gone along when people imitated Ollie.

Jake thought of Roald and Mai Britt.

He wished no one else was in the whole world except himself and the two of them.

But when he really thought about it, he knew that he would miss Sara and Karl, and maybe even Julie, because sometimes she could be nice too.

# Thirty-one

Don't look at the basement door.

Run silently upstairs. Don't step on the brown spot.

Rush past witch Andersen's door.

Hold your breath going by the spooks' door where something is standing with ears listening and listening and listening.

Get past Karlsen.

Then he was home.

Dad wasn't there. Not this time either.

Jake went to his room, but he didn't dare stay there, even though it was light outside, because he heard the birds scratching at the closet door.

He hurried out again.

Jake met Dad on the stairs.

"Hi," said Dad. "You going out?"

"No," Jake answered, "I'm coming in."

"So I see," laughed Dad, turning him around. "Then you have to go this way."

Mom was tired when she came home. She was bitter about the customers who made a lot of fuss and trouble and didn't buy anything. Her legs ached, and she felt sure she wouldn't be up to working tomorrow.

"Did you go see Fritz today?" she asked after they were sitting down and eating.

Dad looked down. "No," he mumbled.

"Why not?" Mom was a little angry. "He was expecting you."

Dad shrugged.

Mom didn't say anything more but Jake noticed she was upset.

Dad and Jake did the dishes while Mom lay down to rest. Dad made coffee, and he'd bought pastries.

Mom was in a serious mood when she got up.

They ate the pastries in silence, and Jake felt that

something was about to happen. He held his juice glass tightly with both hands.

"We have to have a talk," said Mom.

Dad didn't answer.

Jake sat very still waiting to be sent out of the room. He almost hoped that would happen, because it was always so awful when the grown-ups had a serious talk. They got angry so easily.

"Erik, if only I could understand why you didn't go see Fritz. After all, he was sitting there waiting for you. He wants to try to help. I think your nerves are getting worse and worse and I think that might be because you don't have anything to do."

Dad put down his coffee cup. He said nothing.

"And wasn't it our plan that I'd go back to school when you started working this autumn? But look what happened. I can't go on much longer because I'm wearing myself out and not making much money. I've got much too much to do. Not only the store, you know, but I have to do too much at home. You often just disappear or forget what has to be done. I really can't take it any longer. You've got to go to Fritz to at least talk with him. If you don't get a job, we'll have to make another arrangement, because this won't work anymore."

She looked at Dad. Her voice was low and calm. Jake was glad that she didn't sound angry.

"I'm waiting for you to say something, Erik."

Dad looked at her. "Linda, it's so awful when you talk this way. Of course I know that you're wearing yourself out for us and having a hard time making ends meet. I'm really sorry that I'm so little help, but my nerves—"

Mom interrupted him. "Then at least you have to take any help that you can."

"I don't know what to do," said Dad. "The very thought of going back to that school and teaching makes me feel sick and sweaty. I can't do it!"

"Then you have to find something else to do," said Mom equally calmly.

"Like what?"

"You must have some idea yourself, don't you? I can't simply decide for you."

"I don't expect that either," Dad replied quietly. "But it's so hard—."

"Tomorrow you have to go see Fritz," said Mom. "Will you do that?"

"Yes," Dad answered, "I will."

# Thirty-two

In the night Jake was woken up by loud poundings on the closet door.

He was frightened and thought he'd forgotten to lock it. But the key was on the night table.

He lay there a long time listening to the pounding. It sounded as if the birds were breaking out of there.

# Thirty-three

"It's a breeze," said Karl.

Jake said nothing.

"I'll show you."

Karl had his own way of getting money. When his mom hid her money so he couldn't find it, Karl had to get hold of cash some other way.

Karl was lucky, lots of people felt sorry for him because he could look so helpless when he wanted to. That helped him get money.

Karl looked down the street.

"See, over there," he said to Jake. "Here comes the right type. You have to look for them. Old ladies with big handbags, or old men with no hats and no brief-cases. They should really have gray hair, because then you know they're old."

An elderly man without a hat or a briefcase, but with gray hair, was coming toward them down the street. He was carrying a full shopping bag in one hand. He looked nice.

"That's important too," said Karl.

When the man had come close enough, Karl put his hands over his eyes and started to cry. At the same time somehow he shrank—it seemed to Jake that he grew smaller.

Jake was surprised by him: Karl cried exactly as if he were really crying.

The man came right over to them, and Karl bawled extra hard.

Then he looked up at the man. "Please help me," he sobbed.

"What's wrong, my boy?" said the man, stopping. Something had also happened to Karl's voice. It had become more childish, and he wasn't using any bad words.

"The big guys—stole—my money—and—now—I don't dare—go—home, 'cause—they'll think—I took it myself—and that I'm blaming the others," sobbed Karl, rubbing his eyes. "An'—now—the guys—are standing

—around that corner—waiting—for me. They—they'll beat me up."

He bawled and bawled.

"But what can I do?" asked the man, looking concerned.

"Let me come with you—around the corner, and—let me stay with you tonight—'cause I don't dare—go home. My Dad—will beat me to death."

"Young fellow," said the man, "this is terrible. How much money did they take?"

"Ten crowns," said Karl, "and I was supposed to buy bread and milk."

The man looked at him awhile.

Then he said, "Well, I usually don't do things like this, but here's ten crowns. Now you won't have to get scolded. You can walk home some other way so the boys don't get you."

Jake didn't believe his eyes. The man handed over ten crowns. It couldn't be that easy. But Karl had been clever, that was a fact. Jake had almost believed him himself. Karl looked completely helpless, standing there sobbing.

Karl took the bills. "Oh, thank you!" he said politely, bobbing his head.

He took a few steps, then turned and grinned.

"I didn't have cash for cigarettes, you see!" he shouted and set off running.

Jake followed.

"Damn kid!" the man shouted after him.

Karl only laughed and thought it didn't matter.

"But," he said later, "it's hard to get money this way. Adults aren't particularly nice, they don't always want to help a poor, helpless little kid. Would you believe it?"

# Thirty-four

"It's all really true," said Jake. "Sara told me after she saw him."

They were standing in the entry: Sara, Karl, Tommy, Julie, and Tora.

Karl had heard about the murderer in the basement. He wanted to find out if it was true.

Sara nodded. "I'm not a liar!" she said. "I saw him!"

"Well, then, go in there and get him," said Karl.

"No," said Sara.

"Why not?" said Karl.

"Because I'm not allowed in there," said Sara.

Karl looked around.

"Jake can go," he said. "It's his basement."

"Right," said the others, looking at him. "It's your basement."

Oh no, he couldn't do that.

"It's not my basement," he said. "I've never been there. Not even once."

"Then, it's about time," said Tommy.

He and Karl each took one of Jake's arms and dragged him over near the door to the basement.

Jake fought as hard as he could, but it didn't do any good. The others came up behind him and pushed.

They stood in the entry hall.

"Do you have the key to the basement?" asked Tommy.

Jake shook his head.

"He's lying," said Sara. "His apartment key will fit the basement door too."

"You just go in there," said Karl, "and come out with proof the murderer's there."

Jake just couldn't. He could feel tears and pee coming. He was going to die on the threshold.

Sara looked at him and whispered so that everyone could hear her, "You have to bring us out some blood to show the murderer's there."

"And an arm," said Tommy.

"Or a head," Karl whispered with bright eyes.

Tora grabbed Julie's hand and pressed up close to her.

"I had to stand here a long time before I saw him," said Sara in a low voice. "I stood exactly where I'm standing now. I looked at the door. A long, long time. I looked and looked. I knew he had to come up in the end, because he sure wanted to find out who was staring so hard at the basement door. Then up he came."

She lowered her voice even more. Karl shoved Jake forward until he stood a couple of steps in front of the others.

"Then the door slowly opened. It creaked and groaned. The crack in the door got wider and wider."

Now Sara was just whispering.

Jake felt himself turn cold all down the back of his neck.

Tora giggled.

"And then," said Sara, "a shadow came out of the door and a head poked out. It was the shadow . . ."

She couldn't get any further.

They all stood there staring. As if frozen to the spot.

For there in front of them the door was slowly opening. It creaked a little but didn't screech. Slowly the crack in the door got wider and wider. A shadow emerged from the door and a head poked out.

Someone screamed; then they all screamed.

Sara and Julie and Tora and Karl and Tommy.

Jake didn't scream. He tried, but he couldn't even make a little peep.

Suddenly they were all running on top of each other, jamming their way through the front door, almost not getting out.

Jake stayed where he was. He couldn't move. His legs felt stuck to the floor.

Tears were welling up. Now I'm dying, he thought.

"What's all this commotion?" said a thundering voice. The shadow looked at him.

Karlsen.

"Is it you?" said Jake, relieved, and his feet came unstuck from the floor. It was the first time he felt happy to see Karlsen.

"Did—did you see the murderer down there?" asked Jake.

Karlsen looked at him from under his bristling eyebrows. "The murderer? What nonsense are you kids up to now? There was no one down there but me."

Jake just looked at him.

"I wouldn't stand here and lie to you about such serious things," said Karlsen. "Murder! Have you ever heard such rubbish! And in our basement." He snorted, standing above Jake on the stairs.

Jake stood where he was. He closed his eyes. He couldn't remember ever being so happy.

Sara had lied. Imagine that!

Then he realized that he had peed in his pants.

It was embarrassing to go home like that but Mom didn't ask why he'd done it.

She was nice that way.

# Thirty-five

It was Sara's turn to have a hard time.

She said it was true. There had been a murderer in the basement, but no one believed her.

"I hate you!" she shouted, and ran off.

Sara hated a lot of things.

She hated boys who wanted to fight, and boys who ran off when she wanted to fight.

She hated dark rye bread with goat cheese because that was what she got to eat every day.

She hated brothers who called her bad names and stole their mom's money and cigarettes.

She hated babies bawling in baby carriages and birds in cages, because they were dumb.

She hated layer cake with cream filling and girls who acted too special to get their hands dirty.

She hated adults who asked dumb questions.

But there was one thing she liked.

Dogs.

Big dogs with thick, thick fur.

She wished she had a big dog all her own that no one else could borrow.

# Thirty-six

It was terribly quiet while they ate supper.

Mom looked at Dad when he wasn't looking at her.

Dad looked at Mom when she wasn't looking at him.

Jake noticed it and got so he didn't feel like eating.

Finally Mom asked, "What did Fritz say today?"

"I didn't talk with him," answered Dad, who went on eating.

Mom put down her knife and fork and left the table. She shut the bedroom door with a little slam.

Jake and Dad were left sitting there without looking at each other.

At last Jake looked at Dad, but Dad pretended he wasn't there.

In the night Jake was woken up by the night birds screaming and clawing at the closet door.

He covered his ears and screamed too.

Then Mom was there. She put her arms around him and whispered quietly.

"There, there," she whispered into his hair. "Everything's going to be all right, really, you'll see."

And the birds slowly fell to rest.

# Thirty-seven

The next day Jake sat in school and couldn't manage to keep up properly. He had so much on his mind.

Suddenly right in the middle of class he felt really terrible. He raised his hand, and the teacher looked over at him questioningly.

And then it happened. He said the terrible thing that got everyone howling with laughter. It was the worst thing that had happened to him in a long time, even worse than the night birds and the murderer in the basement.

"Mommy," he said, "can I have permission to go out?"

They started laughing before he'd finished speaking.

"Mommy! Mommy!" they all shouted at once. "Did you hear? Jake called her Mommy! Jake's in love with his teach–er! Wow, what about that?"

Jake wished he were dead, that he would fall through the floor out of sight, or that he were strong and could beat them all up at once, that he could put a sponge down each of their throats, one after the other.

His teacher laughed too. He saw her white teeth. They were nasty. Until then he'd always thought they looked nice.

He got up and dashed out of the classroom. Way down the corridor he could hear them laughing and calling, "Mommy, Mommy!"

He ran all the way home.

Now he'd never go back to school again for the rest of his life.

"Hey, wow, Mommy!"

How could he say such a thing!

# Thirty-eight

Julie was the one who brought over his schoolbag after school, since he'd run off without it.

Jake was surprised when he opened the door and saw she was the person who'd rung the bell.

At first he was about to slam the door, because he thought she'd come to tease him.

"Your schoolbag," she said, holding it out toward the opening of the door.

He took it without saying anything. He didn't even dare look at her. Then she'd surely just start laughing.

Jake looked down.

"It doesn't matter that you said that," she said. "It was just so funny."

"I know," said Jake angrily.

"Anyhow, I'm not laughing now," said Julie.

True. She wasn't laughing. She didn't giggle once.

"Take care," she said, running downstairs.

She hadn't been mean to him. She hadn't laughed. And she hadn't stepped on his toes either.

Jake felt confused.

This was a Julie he didn't know.

# Thirty-nine

Mai Britt stood on the sidewalk.

Jake saw her from the living room window.

She stood there in her red coat, green scarf, and green cap.

Several people had started wearing scarves and caps to school now, so Mai Britt didn't look as strange anymore. Jake wondered why she just stood there doing nothing. Perhaps she wasn't looking at anything either.

He tried to find out whether her eyes were closed, but that was impossible to see in the dusk of evening.

His arm twitched; he didn't dare. Then he did. He raised his arm and waved several times.

Mai Britt stood still. She probably hadn't seen it.

But then she raised her arm and carefully waved back.

Jake bolted away from the window. He was embarrassed. He never would have dreamt that Mai Britt was watching his window!

And he had waved!


# Forty

Tommy and Karl were standing outside.

"Are you with us?" asked Karl.

Jake just looked at him. He usually didn't get to go along with them when those two were together, because he was too young.

"Great," nodded Tommy.

He would be allowed to go along!

"What's up?" he asked happily.

"Off to the department store to swipe something," said Tommy.

"Swipe?"

"Yep, swipe," said Karl, tossing a half-smoked cigarette away on the sidewalk. An elderly man glared at him angrily, but didn't say anything.

"Come along and we'll see if you dare."

Of course he dared. He dared anything when he was with Tommy and Karl.

There were always a lot of people in the store, but in the afternoon there was an extra amount of rushing and pushing and shoving.

"The best time to go is in the afternoon," said Karl. "Specially Fridays."

Jake didn't like to go in big stores. He always felt he was going to disappear among all the people.

Whenever he was in the supermarket, he was sure one of the big shopping carts would run him over and no one would notice.

"We'd better be careful," said Tommy. "They keep a close watch on kids in the store."

"That's unfair," said Karl. "Just because we're kids, they think we're going to do something crazy."

They took the escalator up to the toy department on the third floor.

"No one will notice us here," said Tommy. "If there's anything you want, just take it."

They went around between the different counters looking at what was on display. At least the others did, but Jake hardly glanced at anything, he was just plain too nervous. Tommy and Karl stopped here and there, picked up toys, and inspected them carefully.

"Now you'll see how easy it is," Karl whispered to Jake.

Tommy and Karl went over to a counter where there were lots of small toys. Very little dolls and tiny, furry teddy bears, miniature cars and doll's furniture.

Tommy and Karl stood looking at the miniature cars. Jake stood a way behind them, he didn't dare go right over there.

"Have you got any miniature Fords?" he suddenly heard Tommy ask a woman who walked past wearing a pink apron.

"Yes, I believe so," she said. "Didn't you find any with the other cars there?"

"No," said Tommy. "There are none here."

"Let's see," said the woman, squatting down and opening a cupboard door under the counter.

Karl glanced quickly around, and suddenly Jake saw him stick two miniature cars in his pocket.

Tommy had squatted down beside the saleswoman. She was hunting around in some boxes.

Karl sat down beside them, and right after that Tommy stood up.

"There," said Karl, "isn't that a Ford on that box in there?"

The woman stuck her head almost into the cupboard to see. Tommy squatted down again in the same place. His jacket pocket bulged with a little teddy bear.

"Yes, you're right," said the saleswoman, taking out the box. "Here are the Fords."

"Fine," said Karl. "Someone's bound to come along and want one soon."

"But don't you want one?" said the woman, somewhat sourly.

"No," said Tommy. "We just wanted to tell you there weren't any Fords here."

They got up and left.

The woman watched them go with a resigned expression on her face. Then she opened the box and put a number of miniature Fords in the pile of cars that was now two cars smaller.

They stopped next to the down escalator.

"It's as easy as that when you know how," said Tommy.

"Well," said Karl.

"Well," said Tommy.

Both of them looked at him.

"Now it's your turn," said Karl.

His turn. Did they mean that he—? Oh, no. Not that.

"Well," said Karl. "Are you chicken?"

He sure was.

He looked at Karl, whose eyes weren't kind anymore. They were angry. Jake realized he couldn't get out of this. He thought about the bad time lots of young kids on the street had because Karl and Tommy and some other big boys were mean to them. Jake had been lucky —so far.

Karl's eyes told him what it would be like for him if he didn't do what Karl said.

Jake gulped and gulped.

He was forced to do it, because he didn't want to be tormented like Henrik and Ollie.

Karl smiled at him. "Clever boy." He was like an adult talking to a small child.

Where should he go?

What should he take?

He had to go where the most people were and take the easiest thing.

Then he caught sight of a red coat, a green scarf, and a green cap disappearing up the escalator with a brown coat.

Wasn't that . . . ?

Jake hurried over to the escalator and followed them. Karl and Tommy followed him.

It was Mai Britt and her mother. They got off the escalator at the third floor. Jake followed, Karl and Tommy too.

Mai Britt and her mother stopped at the perfume department. Her mother went over to a counter and spoke to a saleswoman.

Mai Britt went off a little way on her own and stopped to look at something in a box. Handkerchiefs. They were small and pink—you could almost see through them— and they had white flowers embroidered in one corner.

Mai Britt picked one up and looked at it a long time before she put it back in the box and went over to her mother.

Jake knew what he wanted to take.

He started sweating and his knees shook. He could feel the blood pounding in his head.

He went over to the box, but in a way it wasn't he who went there.

He didn't see anything except the box and the word *handkerchief* buzzed and whirled around in his head.

He could feel his hand reach out and take a pink handkerchief.

He felt himself putting it in his pocket.

He heard Karl and Tommy say something, and then it was as if they ran away.

He heard a voice beside him.

"So you want a handkerchief?"

He looked up—and woke up.

A blond woman with red lips and blue eyelids was looking at him. She smiled, but her eyes were mean.

Jake shook his head. Tears came before he was able to stop them.

The woman's eyes turned different, sort of friendlier.

"No," whispered Jake. "I have to— "

He couldn't get any more words out.

The woman leaned down to him. "What do you have to do?"

He shook his head. The handkerchief was like a stone in his pocket.

His fingers closed around it and lifted it out. He put it back in the box. His fingers started to tingle afterward.

The woman stood silently looking at him. Then she nodded slowly.

"Yes, I think you're right," she said.

Then she turned and walked back to a counter a short distance away that Jake hadn't noticed. He had seen nothing but the box.

Jake dried the tears with the back of his hand.

Karl and Tommy had disappeared. He was alone.

He turned.

A red coat, a green scarf, and a green cap stood right in front of him.

He started. It was Mai Britt.

They looked at each other.

Her eyes were big and solemn.

His were small and red from crying.

She had seen it all.

Jake ran past her and out just as fast as he could. He could never, never look at Mai Britt again. Not in school or on the street.


# Forty-one

"Crybaby!"

Karl tossed away his cigarette butt and glared at him. Glared angrily.

Jake and Karl were sitting under the bushes near the biggest oak tree. Fortunately Tommy wasn't there.

Jake didn't speak.

"You're just a baby," said Karl. "Who'd believe you're in second grade. First time, and you get caught! I've never been caught yet, ever. I'm even better than lots of the older guys, in fact."

Jake felt that Karl was growing before his very eyes, turning into a hero.

"It wasn't nice that you two split," Jake mumbled.

"God!" exclaimed Karl. "You can't have wanted us to get caught too, Tommy and me. We hadn't even swiped anything from that box."

"You could've said you were going," said Jake.

"The woman was right there, and then it was too late, chicken," said Karl. "No, you're really too young and scared to be up to serious stuff like that. And handkerchiefs, for God's sake!"

"What about you!" Jake got angry. "All you took was some little cars. You don't even play with cars."

"Shut up!"

Karl suddenly leapt on him. Jake felt sharp twigs hit around his ears. Then he was down on the ground with Karl on top of him.

"Now, don't say so many dumb things," said Karl.

Jake didn't answer.

"Okay," said Karl. "You'll get one more chance, but only if you go in alone and come out with what we tell you to take. Get that? Otherwise you can't be with us."

"I don't want to be with you," said Jake.

"You're crazy," said Karl. "Don't want to be with us?"

Jake tried to get up but Karl was sitting hard on his stomach.

"You know, some of the kids around here have a hard time. Right?" asked Karl.

"Yes," mumbled Jake.

"Well, you're going to have a hard time too," said Karl. "Now, you don't want that, do you?"

"No," said Jake.

"Well, then, you have to go along with us, you know. You have to do what we say."

"No," said Jake.

Karl sighed. "I never would have thought you're so dumb."

He stood up. Jake got back up on his feet again. He went off without looking around.

Karl shouted after him. "I'll let you know when you get your chance."


# Forty-two

In the night he dreamt about handkerchiefs with red eyes and black wings that chased him, screaming and shrieking.

Then Mom was there again.

"What's wrong?" she asked, concerned.

He shook his head.

Nothing.

Just a dream.

# Forty-three

He went to school on Monday.

No one said anything about his having gone home in the middle of the day.

No one laughed.

Twice he thought he heard someone say "Mommy" behind him in the school yard, but when he turned to see, he didn't know who it could have been.

It was almost as if what happened on Friday hadn't happened.

Either they had decided in school that they weren't going to talk about it, or else he'd dreamed that it had happened.

# Forty-four

The rain started again in the afternoon. It got dark quickly. Under the asphalt on the street there seemed to be a glittering light. He had a heavy feeling in his stomach and he thought, "Now I'm sinking into the street." But it was only the light and the rain.

He walked in the park while he waited for Mom. Dad had said again that he was going to talk with Fritz, but he hadn't come home yet.

In the park suddenly, yellow and red leaves were lying on the ground. He hadn't seen them yesterday. Perhaps that was because of the windy rain today that had brought real fall weather.

Jake stopped and looked at a yellow-brown leaf lying in the middle of the asphalt path. He looked and looked until a new leaf came down on top of the first one.

Then he walked on.

The rain sighed through the branches and pattered against the leaves. He could see the wind tug at the trees and pull off leaves.

No kids were playing in the playground. The sand-box was wet and ugly. A truck someone had forgotten lay on its side half-buried in sand. A red plastic bucket stood collecting autumn rain.

He walked on. Shuffled through the wet, green grass. The streetlamps along the asphalt path didn't shine out into the dark center of the lawn where the big trees grew.

Jake wasn't scared. He could see the streetlamps and lights in the houses and from cars, and the dark shadows of people on the sidewalks.

He came to the big thicket where Karl usually hid. He wasn't there now. Jake walked around the bushes to see from the back.

Then he noticed something strange. He wasn't absolutely sure, but he felt there was someone on the other side of the bushes.

Jake stopped and listened.

Rain and wind, sighing in the branches. He couldn't hear anything else.

Then he took a step again, and instantly the feeling was there once more.

Someone was walking on the other side who did not want to be discovered!

Jake did not get frightened. Something told him that whoever was on the other side was even more scared than he was.

Jake ran fast around the bushes. There was no one there.

What could that mean?

He crept into the bushes carefully and tried to see in among the branches but that was impossible. He saw only leaves and shadows and shiny wet branches.

He leaned down and looked around a bush, and then he was almost sure that he saw something dark disappear behind the curtain of leaves some distance away.

Jake crept on stealthily but didn't find whoever was hiding from him.

At last he gave up. The other person didn't want to be seen.

A mystery.

Who was sneaking around not wanting to be seen?

It couldn't be just the wind and the rain.

It was something else.

Maybe it was the autumn—

# Forty-five

Jake slipped into the apartment and locked the door. What had happened in the park still sat deep inside him, making him be silent.

Mom and Dad were sitting in the living room. They hadn't heard him, but Jake heard their voices.

Mom was the one talking. He couldn't hear what she was saying. The door was pulled almost closed.

Her voice was low like when she was comforting someone.

Then he heard Dad, but he wasn't saying anything. Jake heard only a crying sound.

Dad was crying.

It was such a long time since he'd heard Dad sobbing that he'd forgotten when it was.

A weird feeling came over Jake.

The door was closed. Closed to him. He wasn't supposed to hear this. They had closed him out.

He stood awhile looking at the door. Then he turned and quietly closed the front door behind him.

He went down the stairs with a lump that grew and grew in his stomach.

When he was almost all the way down, he had to sit on the stairs. His stomach was in a knot.

He rested his head on the banister and closed his eyes.

Then he realized that he had sat down right on the brown spot.

"Abracadabra." He couldn't get the word out. It was too late anyway, he'd already been sitting on the spot for a while.

It was as if it didn't matter. His head had no more room for any more terrible thoughts after having heard

Mom and Dad in the living room and seeing the closed door.

He gave up. Just sat there waiting for the awful thing that might happen because he'd sat down on the brown spot.

# Forty-six

The terrible thing happened.

The most terrible thing that could happen.

He recognized the voice and squeezed his eyelids tighter shut. If only it were something he imagined, but the hand on his arm was real.

Witch Andersen leaned over him.

"What is the matter, dear?" she said.

Jake didn't answer. He couldn't answer. He didn't want to answer. He didn't dare answer.

"Something seems to be wrong," she said over his head.

He caught a glimpse of her eyes and saw her neat white hair.

That was just something she put on to look nice, said Sara.

Her eyes were blue and gentle.

They were only glass eyes, said Sara. Underneath she really had black, glowing coals instead of eyes.

Her face had many crisscrossed wrinkles and it looked as if her whole face were smiling.

That's only a mask, said Sara. Her face was really made of glass. It was smooth and hard so she couldn't smile.

"Would you like to come with me and have a cup of hot chocolate?" she said. "I baked muffins today too."

He didn't want to, but if he said no, she was bound to send him right through the worn brown spot to the place that was nowhere. Sara said she could do that.

"Come," she said, getting her key out of her purse.

She went up the stairs, and Jake followed. He had to. She had power over him; he couldn't get away.

The witch put her key in the lock and opened the door.

Jake thought he heard a terrified bat flapping around inside the place and he thought he saw red eyes vanish into the darkness.

"Please, come in," she said, stepping aside to let him in first.

Jake wished someone would come by on the stairs. Someone who could rescue him.

What if Mom or Dad suddenly realized what terrible danger their son was in. They'd come running with tears streaming, crying hysterically.

And then the door would close behind him the moment they got there.

And he'd stand listening to Mom and Dad pounding on the door, sobbing "Jake, Jake!" while the witch cackled (because of course all witches do that).

He walked into her front hall. The door closed behind him. No one came by on the stairs.

It was probably the last time he would see the brown spot and the stairs and everything.

He was willing to do just about anything to get out again. He'd steal a hundred thousand handkerchiefs and get sent to jail just to avoid being put in her cage.

"Go right on in to the living room and sit down," she said. "I'll hurry and heat up the chocolate."

Jake walked into the living room.

It was nice in there. He hadn't thought it would be like that. Witches should have mean, ugly places, but here there was a sofa, a table and chairs, and flower-printed curtains and pictures of serious people in round frames on the walls.

There was no cage.

Where was it?

Jake hurried out into the hall. Then she appeared immediately.

"I have to p—pee," he stammered.

"It's the door with the heart on it," she said, smiling.

He hesitated before he went in, and leaned against the door.

There was no cage in the bathroom, which was white with red pipes. It was nice in there too.

He came out. The door next to it stood ajar. He peeked in quickly. A lamp was lit on a night table. No sign of a cage.

"It's in the middle of the living room," Sara had said, but that wasn't true.

He went back into the living room and sat on the very edge of a chair.

Over in one corner stood a chest with—he thought it wasn't true—toys.

He had to go over and look at them.

Teddy bears, cars, blocks—

"Those are my grandchild's toys," said the witch, who'd come in without his noticing her. "He comes here so often that he always keeps these toys here."

A grandchild, how strange.

"Do come sit on the sofa. Your chocolate will get cold fast."

She had poured a big cup for him. Next to the cup was a plate piled with brown muffins.

"Now, just eat," she said.

He thought of Snow White and the apple and didn't dare. Witch Andersen had to help herself first. After that he took the muffin that was right next to the one she'd taken. He had to reach across to the other side of the plate to get it.

"It's so much fun to have children in the house," she

said while she chewed her muffin with raisins in it. "You're the only child here in this entry except for the Rudds' little fellow. I miss the sound of children," she said. "That's why it's so nice that I have a grandson who comes to visit now and then. He makes such a racket that I'm afraid he disturbs the neighbors, but no one complains, so I hope they're not annoyed at me."

Jake discovered that he'd eaten the muffin.

Her voice was kind, and he could hear that she wasn't pretending.

Suddenly she got serious. "There's something I have to ask you," she said, looking at him with her mild, blue eyes. "I have a feeling that you are avoiding me. You run every time you see me. I'd really like to know if I did something wrong or if I frightened you. I'd like to straighten things out if I could. I just want to be friendly with people."

Jake blushed, but said nothing.

"I'd hate to have anyone feel I'm mean or threatening or anything like that," she said.

Sara had said that as soon as she got inside her door, her apron fell off her and she simply turned right into a witch, but that wasn't true. Jake thought of the murderer in the basement. He hadn't known that Sara was so mean as to lie. This was the second time.

"You know," said Mrs. Andersen, "it would be fun for me if you'd come visit sometimes. I've got lots of toys and books you might enjoy, so if you feel like it, just come again."

Jake looked down the whole time.

"I can see that something is the matter," she said. "I won't ask what it is. You can tell me yourself if you want to. Would you like some more chocolate?"

Jake heard that he said, "Yes, thank you."

He wasn't scared of her anymore.

Sara. If he were strong, he would beat her up because she said such mean things about other people.

Mrs. Andersen, he thought. She must have some other name in front of Andersen too. Bodil or Lisa or something. Perhaps he'd find out sometime.

# Forty-seven

When Jake got into bed and Mom came in to see him, he had to ask why Dad had been crying.

Mom sat down on the edge of the bed. "He went to see Fritz today, who said he thought Dad ought to try to work again. Dad said it wasn't the middle of October yet, but Fritz had found out about a school where he knew the headmaster and asked whether they might need a substitute teacher for a few hours. So Dad will go to work right away—tomorrow."

"Tomorrow?" said Jake.

"Tomorrow," said Mom. "Fritz said the best thing was to plunge right in. Dad will have a seventh grade class, and perhaps that'll be better than high school. Let's hope."

That night Jake didn't hear the birds.

# Forty-eight

Dad wasn't hungry at breakfast next morning.

"You should eat," said Mom with concern.

He shook his head and picked up his coffee cup. His hand shook. Coffee sloshed out onto the table.

Dad looked at Jake. "I'm starting school again today," he said, and Jake saw that his eyes were red.

# Forty-nine

"I never said Mrs. Andersen was a witch," said Sara.

"Yes, you did," said Jake. "You've said it a million times."

Sara sighed. "Your hearing's really crazy. You should

ask for new ears for Christmas. Did you see Andersen when you were there?"

"Andersen?" Jake looked at her, startled.

"Yes, Andersen," said Sara.

"No." Jake shook his head.

"There, you see," said Sara triumphantly.

"See what?" Jake didn't understand anything.

"Andersen is the one who's a sorcerer," Sara whispered, moving really close to Jake.

He didn't like it when she did that, because it felt creepy when Sara spoke right into his ear.

"And you know, when people go there, she shuts him into a closet in the bedroom after she's gagged and bound him. He can only get out if he changes himself into a black poodle. But he almost never does that, because that's hard to manage."

Jake looked at her with big eyes.

Then he thought of the murderer in the basement.

He thought of Mrs. Andersen who was not a witch.

"That's not true," he said.

"Yes," said Sara.

"It's stupid," said Jake.

"Watch out you don't get a beating," said Sara. "It's true."

Jake kept quiet. He didn't want to get beat up by Sara. It was best to pretend that he believed it was true.

# Fifty

Jake didn't dare go home after school. He wandered around and talked a little with Sara and watched out for Karl and Tommy.

When the clothes shop where Mom worked closed for the day he was standing there.

Today he didn't feel up to being home with Dad. Dad's eyes had frightened Jake that morning.

"My goodness, you're standing here!" said Mom when she came out. "You could've come inside to wait."

It had started to rain a little, and he had that sinking feeling in his stomach and the asphalt glittered with light.

"Have you been home?" asked Mom.

"No," said Jake.

Mom walked fast, and Jake almost had to run to keep up with her.

"Do you think Dad is home?" he asked after a while.

"Why shouldn't he be?" replied Mom lightly.

Jake realized that she was acting. She was pretending. She didn't want to frighten him, because she was worried herself.

"He's gone away a lot," said Jake.

"But today he started school again," said Mom. "He's probably home."

Still, Jake could hear that she was worried.

Dad was home. He had cooked supper. Fried pollack and onions.

"Hello," said Mom. "How good you're here."

Dad smiled at them.

They ate without saying a word. It was as if they were waiting for something, something from Dad. Mom sort of didn't dare ask how it had gone.

But at last it came out.

"How did it go today?" she asked casually as she took another potato.

"Fine," replied Dad, but he didn't look up.

Mom and Jake glanced quickly at each other.

Jake couldn't manage the rest of his supper.

# Fifty-one

The evening was black and wet.

Jake stood still on the sidewalk looking at the house where he lived.

Warm yellow light in the living room window.

Suddenly someone was standing next to him. He didn't turn, just felt that someone was there.

He knew who it was.

He had dreaded this, but still he wasn't scared when it finally happened.

Neither of them spoke.

He felt something against his hand, in his hand. It was one finger, two fingers, a whole hand.

He was standing holding someone's hand.

Jake held Mai Britt's hand. Or she was holding his hand.

"Thanks," she said quietly.

He had never heard her voice before. It was neat too.

"Thanks for the handkerchief."

"You didn't get it," replied Jake.

"No, but I figured out what you meant."

The woman came to the window.

Quickly Mai Britt let go of his hand and moved aside.

The woman just stood looking awhile. Jake looked back, but he couldn't see her face. It was only a black blob on the third floor.

The window closed again.

"She can see me," said Mai Britt.

Jake heard her footsteps as she crossed the street and disappeared into the doorway of Number Thirty-seven.

# Fifty-two

Right before Jake was supposed to go to bed, it started to rain. The drops rattled against the windowpanes.

Dad stood by the window looking at the rivulets of rain that ran down the glass.

"Come," he said to Jake. "Let's take a walk in the rain."

"It's really bedtime," said Mom.

"Almost bedtime," said Dad. "Just a little walk in the rain. Won't you come along, Linda?"

Mom looked at him, then she nodded.

Boots and slickers came out. Yellow and red and orange. The red one was Jake's.

It was wonderful to go outside. The rain was coming down in thick, gray streaks against the park.

No people were out. A couple of cars splashed water far in onto the sidewalk.

Mom and Dad and Jake were alone in the world.

They took each other's hands and ran across the street into the park.

The rain was coming from the southwest; drumming sounds in their ears. Rain rattled against their rain gear and rasped against the leaves and sighed through the treetops, which were more and more bare every day.

The streetlamps had wet yellow circles of light and the grass was a wet sea that stretched to the end of the world.

Jake looked at Dad.

Dad laughed and his face was wet and good to look at.

Mom's rain smile. Her long hair was loose on top of her rain jacket gathering raindrops.

They ran across the lawn. Water splashed over their boots.

"We're falling to earth with the rain!" shouted Dad, swinging Jake around. "We're rain, rain, rain! When it stops raining, we'll stop running, too."

"Hush!" said Mom. "Listen!"

They stood still and let it all pour and patter down over and around them.

Good sounds. It ran down their backs and tickled on their stomachs.

Walking slowly, they left the wet pools of light and moved toward the shadowy bushes.

No one said anything; they just listened to the rain chatter.

They walked close by the bushes where Karl usually sat. If he'd been there then, he would certainly have run off, Jake thought, laughing a little at the idea of Karl swept away in the middle of a huge flood of rain.

Suddenly Jake stopped and looked behind him.

Dad and Mom stopped too. Dad looked at Jake, but didn't say anything.

"Why did you stop?" Mom asked.

Jake didn't answer. He stared. Right now he could only see bushes and shadows and shiny branches. But it seemed as if someone was waiting for him behind the bushes. As if someone had said his name.

Jake knew who it was. It was the mystery person who had hidden from him a few evenings before.

He took a few steps toward the bushes.

Dad grabbed him again. "Don't do that," he said. "It's so easy to frighten someone when it's dark."

"What do you see?" said Mom.

"There's a boy behind the bushes," whispered Jake, "as big as me."

"But then, he shouldn't be out this late," said Mom. "Let's find out if anything's wrong."

Dad looked toward the bushes. "Hey, boy!" he said not so very loud. "Is there any way we can help you?"

Jake held his breath. What if he answered?

No one answered.

"Of course he doesn't dare say anything," said Mom.

"I'm not dangerous," said Jake so low that no one heard him. "You should know that."

"We ought to find out about this," said Mom. "Let's each of us go a different way around the bushes and then we'll surely see him."

Mom and Jake went to one side, Dad the other. They met behind the bushes, but found no boy.

"Maybe you only thought you saw someone," said Mom.

"No, he was here," replied Jake, and he told them that he'd almost seen him once before.

"Well, he isn't here now, anyway," said Mom.

"Perhaps he's run home and gone to bed," said Dad. "We should do that now, too."

They ran the same way back. Jake between Mom and Dad. They both held his hands.

They ran as if they were part of the rain.

Alone in the world.

But maybe there was also one other little boy.

Jake wasn't sure.

# Fifty-three

Sara was sobbing.

She was trying to hide behind the trash cans at Number Thirty-nine, but she was too big. Her legs stuck out, and besides, she was not exactly crying silently.

Julie and Tora stood listening to her. They had never known that Sara could cry.

Tommy passed by and turned in to the yard.

"Who's that?" he asked, pointing to the legs sticking out.

"Sara," said Julie.

"Sara?" said Tommy, astounded. "I don't believe it." He had to go over and look.

"God," he said afterward, "I'd never have believed it."

Jake stood off by himself. Tommy didn't notice him. Julie and Tora had clearly forgotten him.

He was confused. There was something all wrong about Sara crying. He couldn't make sense of it.

It hurt to hear her sob and wail. Now and then her legs twitched.

When Tommy went away again, Jake crept behind the cans.

"Sara," he said quietly, "what is it?"

Usually it was Sara who asked him that.

She shook her head. Her whole body trembled.

"Sara." He didn't know what to do.

She just cried.

He began to crawl away again.

"No," she called, pulling him to her so hard that he almost couldn't get his breath.

Her tears ran down his cheeks as if he were the one crying.

She held onto him hard. His arms hurt. But she didn't let go of him.

"It's—it's Ka—rl," she finally sobbed.

Something about Karl.

"They may come to g–g–get him."

Her voice disappeared in gasps.

"He—he got caught with—with some—of—of the b–big boys in the store."

It was hard to understand what she said.

"—They said he'd been—seen—several times. They came—home—yesterday—and said he—that he couldn't—stay home—anymore. So they—they may come—to—to get—him."

Sara collapsed on top of him, and her head rested in his arms.

Jake didn't know what to do.

"But he's my brother, after all," whispered Sara.

Jake stayed sitting there until she had completely finished crying. Then he got up.

Julie and Tora were still standing there. They looked at him with curiosity when he came out from behind the trash cans, but he pretended not to see them.

He hurried out onto the sidewalk. He didn't know what he could do for Sara.

# Fifty-four

Jake had only three hours of school the next day.

When he unlocked the apartment door, he knew right off that Dad was home.

Something ice cold hit his stomach.

Dad should have been in school teaching then.

Jake didn't dare go into the living room right away.

Dad was sitting in the armchair leafing through a newspaper. He didn't look up when Jake came in.

"Hi," he said into the newspaper, sounding tired.

"Hi," Jake answered with a small voice.

Jake sat down on the edge of the sofa.

"Aren't you in school?" he asked softly.

"No, as you can see," replied Dad, without looking up.

"Oh, right," was all Jake said.

Dad looked at the paper. Jake sat there. He wanted to leave the room, but couldn't get himself up to go.

At last Dad put the paper on the table.

"Jake," he said solemnly, "it won't work. I don't dare. Today I couldn't even make it into the classroom."

There were tears in Dad's eyes, and all around his mouth his skin was trembling.

"I don't know what I'm going to do."

He got up. Walked back and forth across the floor a few times, stared out the window.

"Jake, it won't work."

He went out into the hall.

Jake wanted to ask Dad not to go, but the door closed behind him before he could open his mouth.

# Fifty-five

He was still sitting on the sofa when Mom came home.

"Hello, is anyone home?" she called.

Jake didn't answer.

Mom looked into the living room. "Oh," she said, "you're sitting here."

He looked at her. Her smile, she was happy. He started to cry, couldn't hold it back.

"Jake, sweetheart," said Mom, "what is it?"

And he told her that Dad had been home and what he'd said.

Mom sank down beside him on the sofa. He felt her become little, as if she crumpled.

She took his hand.

"We have to be strong, Jake, you and I," she said quietly. "It's no time to be weak."

"Why is he this way, Mom?"

"He doesn't even know that himself," she answered.

Jake looked at Mom. Around her mouth she looked stern.

"But we have to cope with it, Jake. We have to go on and keep on our feet."

She quickly covered her face with her hands, but she didn't cry. She sat there as if she closed Jake out.

He felt all alone.

# Fifty-six

They had eaten supper. It was dark outside. Dad was still away.

"I'll go out and look for him," said Jake.

"All right," said Mom, "but don't you go away too."

"No," answered Jake with a smile. "I'll come back."

Mai Britt was not standing on the sidewalk.

Jake went into the park. Some kids were in the playground, but they were unusually quiet.

The asphalt paths were deserted. The benches had been removed a couple of days ago. That was to stop winter from sitting down on them, Dad had said. Jake thought that quite funny.

Clogs and a Windbreaker, that was what Dad was wearing again today.

So he was anywhere. Perhaps he wouldn't come home again. Jake was freezing and stuck his hands deeper in his pockets.

He came to the bushes near the oak tree.

There he stopped and listened. Yes, someone was on the other side.

Jake stood still.

He felt something move softly in some branches on the other side, but he couldn't be completely sure.

"I know you're there," he said in a low voice. "I'm not going to hurt you."

Nothing happened.

"I'm looking for my dad," he said. "He's wearing clogs and a Windbreaker."

The silence continued on the other side of the bushes.

"Could you please tell me if you've seen him?"

There was silence. Then he heard something, and a shadow appeared from the bushes. A small shadow, no bigger than himself.

It was a boy. He stopped way inside the bushes. They couldn't see each other clearly, but anyway Jake caught a glint where his eyes should be.

"He's sitting under the big oak over there," the shadow said softly, pointing further into the darkness.

Jake looked at the shadow. He couldn't ask why he was in the bushes. He couldn't ask why he had hidden from him twice, but the shadow was not afraid of him anymore. He was sure of that, otherwise he wouldn't have come out.

"My name is Jake," said Jake.

"My name's Jake," said the other boy.

Really strange. No, it wasn't really so strange after all. It was fine. Jake thought he could see Shadow-Jake smile.

"I've got to get my dad," said Jake.

"Yes," said the other one.

Jake turned to go.

"I'll be here tomorrow too," said Shadow-Jake behind him.

Jake turned back.

"I'll come here tomorrow too," he said.

They looked at each other. It was settled.

Then he walked toward the oak tree farther off in the darkness.

# Fifty-seven

Dad was sitting on the ground with his back against the tree trunk. He was sitting looking down at the ground.

"Dad," said Jake, "come home and be with us."

Dad looked up. "Is that you, Jake?" he said, and sounded glad.

"Come along home," Jake said again.

"I'm only in the way," said Dad. "Everything goes to hell. You have no use for me."

The words hurt Jake. He didn't know what he should say.

"I'm only in the way," repeated Dad. "Linda has much too much to do, and that's my fault. And I can't stay at the school."

"Dad, come along home."

Jake didn't have anything else to say.

Dad sighed and stood up.

"Yes," he said, "I'll come along. I'm a coward, you know. It's cold sitting here, so it'll be good to come in where it's warm."

He took Jake's hand and started to run.

The way they had run that evening when it rained so wonderfully.

And yet, this was different.

# Fifty-eight

All three of them went to bed early.

Jake lay listening to their evening sounds while he looked at the good light in the hallway.

Then there was silence from Mom and Dad's room, and Jake fell asleep.

Weird dreams. Something whizzed and roared over his head. Wings with black feathers.

He saw eyes that glowed in the dark and open, screeching beaks.

Jake wanted to wake up, but sleep held him back.

Suddenly something screamed louder than the birds. Jake sat up wide awake in bed.

It was Dad screaming and screaming.

"Erik!" said Mom. "Erik! Wake up!"

"Turn on the light!" shouted Dad. "The light!"

"There, there," said Mom. "You've been having really bad dreams."

Jake turned on his bedside lamp.

Then he saw that the door to the closet was open. He'd forgotten to lock it last night.

Jake got up and went over to the door with the key. Carefully, he locked the door, and for safety's sake he tugged at the door three times afterward to make sure that it was really locked.

He went in to Mom and Dad's room.

They were sitting up in bed with the light on.

"It's all right now, Dad," said Jake. "I forgot to lock the closet last night, but now I've done it."

Mom looked at him. "You go back to bed, Jake. Dad was only dreaming, you know. It's nothing terrible."

She stroked Dad's hair. "You're worn out, Erik. Lie down and sleep now. We can talk in the morning. You probably had nightmares because of school and everything troubling you."

Dad put his arm around her. "Linda," was all he said.

"There, there," said Mom. "Everything will be all right, you'll see. Tomorrow . . ."

But her voice was worn-out and tired.

# Fifty-nine

Jake lay in bed waiting for sleep.

Tomorrow, said Mom.

Tomorrow there was Mai Britt, he'd decided that.

Tomorrow there was the shadow called Jake.

Tomorrow there was Karl and Sara's tears.

Tomorrow, said Mom.

Jake slept, and the night birds were silent.

Tormod Haugen, born in 1945, is a well-known translator and author of children's books in Norway. One of his books, *Zeppelin*, has been made into a feature film. *The Night Birds* has won many awards, including the German Juvenile Book Award and the Norwegian Children's Book Prize, and has been translated into eight languages.

Sheila La Farge has translated many books from Swedish, Danish, and Norwegian. Her translation of *The Glassblower's Children* by Maria Gripe was on the 1978 Honors List for translation selected by the International Board of Books for Young People. She lives in Cambridge, Massachusetts.